AGHAST

Published by Kraken Press © 2015
Please visit us on the web at www.krakenpress.com

Editors
George Cotronis
Lori Michelle

Assistant Editor
Gordon White

Book Design by George Cotronis
Illustrations © George Cotronis
www.cotronis.com

Rust & Flame created by Brennen Reece
http://www.brennenreece.com/

ISBN: 978-91-979725-4-3

A · GHAST
ADJ.
STRUCK WITH OVERWHELMING SHOCK OR AMAZEMENT: FILLED
WITH SUDDEN FRIGHT OR HORROR

TABLE OF CONTENTS

11   NIGHT-BIRD

24   STICKS AND BONES

32   A MARVELOUS NEUTRALITY

46   PLAGUE MOTHER

50   GREENER PASTURES

58   HAVES AND HAVE NOTS

66   APPEARANCES

82   ROCKPORT BOYS

94   CLEANING UP

108   DEFORMED SON

116   RUST & FLAME

ACKNOWLEDGEMENTS

Thanks to: Gordon White for battling the slush gods with me. To Lori Michelle for her editing prowess and fixing all my mistakes. To Natalia Theodoridou for her invaluable help. To Eugenia Rose, Richard Thomas, Max Booth III, Benoit Lelievre, Konstantine Paradias, Nick Mamatas, Tim Marquitz, J.M. Martin, Phillip Michael Buchan and Ellen Datlow for their support.

To Gemma Files, Jeff Strand, Megan Arkenberg, Aaron Polson, Esther Saxey, Michael Wehunt, Craig D.B. Patton, Leo Norman, Jamie Killen, and Tim Waggoner, for their stories.

To everyone who made Aghast a reality through Kickstarter, and to SFSignal, Starburst Magazine, The Qwillery, My Bookish Ways, and HorrorNews.net, for helping us spread the word.

WITH THANKS TO

Anon, ANIMAfelis, Rebecca J. Allred, Shane Alonso, Rachel Anding, C.B. Auder, Azelma, Kevin Babineau, Jeff Barr, John Beattie, Bill, Anders Bohlin, Ann K. Boyer, John Bowman, Jane Brooks, Marie Cashin, Casey Calouette, Jay Caselberg, Aaron Caskey, Iain Chantler, Joyce Chong, Dylan Clayton, Simone Colombo, Michael Cook, Joshua Crowe, Dana, Brad Dancer, Steve Dempsey, Efthymia Despotaki, John Dimatos, Andrey Dolganov, Scott Dorward, Belinda Draper, Jeremy Dyson, Chris Earl, eilidh, Undead Eskimo, John Garside, Tess Grantham, Michael Griffin, John Gublo, Audrey Hare, Seth Harris, Andrew Hatchell, Jon Hodgson, Erik Homme, Gordon White, Jack, Kyle Johnson, MP Johnson, Joonas Joensuu, Josh Jordan, Jorgan, Josh, David James Keaton, Zakary Kerr, Bob Kimble, Andy Kitkowski, Erlend Thorin Kirkevold, Kirsty Logan, Nicholas Mamatas, Tim Marquitz, Marmæl, J.M. Martin, Alison McBain, Rabeya Merenkov, Marshall Miller, Flavio Mortarino, C.M. Muller, John Stewart Muller, Mumble Mumble, Christopher Niehoff, Nina, Nathan D. Paoletta, Dino Parenti, Rhonda Parrish, Pavel, Tony Peak, David Perlmutter, Michael Pignatella, Joshua Ramsey, Mick Reddick, Michael Richards, Ken Ringwald, David Church Rodríguez, Joseph Sale,

Richard Alan Scott, Konstantinos Thomaidis, Ralf "Sandfox" Sandfuchs, Scoff, Barry Skelhorn, Kenny Soward, Spyros, Cameron Suey, Marc Tetlow, Richard Thomas, Torrain, Scott Virtes, David Alexander Ward, Stephanie McAlea, zalfer.

NIGHT-BIRD

GEMMA FILES

Somewhere in the dark, just at evening, there always seems to be a bird who calls out loudly, sounding betrayed. It's a fierce, braying call. You hear it rise up over the roof-tops, past the power-lines, to graze the lowermost clouds. Orange and pink and red against a dark blue sky, almost navy; dusk never looks like this in the country. In Toronto, though, people just shrug and say *it's the pollution,* as if that's something to be proud of.

Some mornings you wake up with your eyes stinging like you're about to cry, not knowing over what. Some days you look out down Ossington, where the road dips towards the business district and then further still, running straight into the Lake, and see the whole horizon turn sepia as the air takes on a stinging brown tinge: heat haze, exhaust, effluvia of a million different engines, downtown's constant racket. The city, building and rebuilding itself, with nowhere left for it to go but up.

C'mon, though, baby, Levi used to say. *It's good here, right? Better than it ever could've been, if we'd stayed.* And you would nod, smiling: oh yes, yes. Of course it is. Of course.

Where you came from is a shell of a place, operating on half-speed, half-life. No work since the plant shut down, and the summer people don't make up for it. It's a place to drive through, not to live. So Toronto is an improvement, obviously, in almost every way, with no room for debate—not that Levi ever would've brooked any.

You came here two years ago, give or take. Drove all night and part of a day to a buddy's house in Mimico, then camped there 'til the job he'd been promised made you enough for first and last month's rent.

After that it was somewhere further in, Queen West, almost to Roncesvalles. The last streetcar stop before that final highway underpass between city proper and suburban sprawl, where foxes sometimes crept out of the foliage and skunks waddled down the alleyways like fat, crippled cats. Misa and Aaron used to crouch in the front yard of your apartment building, watching fascinated as a steady stream of thumbnail-sized black-lacquer beetles colonized the ruin of a dead stump. Not much else to watch if you didn't count crazy homeless people wandering by, so it wasn't like you blamed them, especially since Levi couldn't afford cable.

It'd have been bearable if you could have both gotten jobs, or if you'd been able to pay someone else to watch Aaron and Misa long enough for you to find one, let alone keep one. Instead, it was you and them stuck inside a tiny no-bedroom or out roaming the streets until Levi came home, unable to stay in coffee-shops more than fifteen minutes at a time, for fear you'd be asked to pay for something. An endless drudgery of maintenance and busywork, scraping together edible meals from whatever was cheapest and trying to keep them quiet when Levi finally started to beat you, so the neighbours wouldn't complain. All of which still holds true, to one degree or another, but at least these days you don't have to do it with one eye blacked, or nursing a cracked rib.

Your first real job in Toronto, therefore—arranged by Miss Sada at the shelter, the still point your life now revolves around—has you cutting and packaging at Abreu's Meats for ten hours a day, six to four, at which point you hand over to Mrs Abreu's son Joao, so he can re-stock and close out. Your landlady Mrs Cambres looks after the kids, one of a loose coven of women—mostly little, mostly older, though it's hard to tell exactly how old—who volunteer at the shelter, running mini-daycares out of their living-rooms for "transitioning" shelter graduates. Misa and Aaron love her, especially when she sings them Portuguese songs about the boogeyman in her low, slightly creaking voice:

Vai-te, Coca. Vai-te, Coca.
Leave, big eater. Leave, eater of children.
Para cima do telhado,
Go to the top of the roof,
Deixa o menino dormir
Um soninho descansado

| Aghast · Book One

12

And let the child have
A quiet sleep.

"Three more months and you can get them into kindergarten, down at Saint Joe's," Mrs Cambres tells you, clucking in refusal when you try to press whatever you can into her hand, at the end of the day. "No, no, away with it! You're gone from that *cahorro,* that's my payment, *doce.* Spend it on candy."

Hunched in her black, her scarf pulled up, those fierce eyes unblinking, round and cataract grey-blue behind their thick-lensed spectacles. She's a lump of a woman, solid from top to bottom, but she moves fast, and silently— almost too silent to hear coming. Appears without warning at your elbow through a haze of fatigue, every afternoon when you come to pick them up, and cocks her head to one side, smiling, her nose like a hooked blade.

"It's hard, isn't it, *doce*?" she asks, sympathetically. "I remember! They can suck the blood right out of you, these little ones, if you let them."

You want to agree, particularly on Monday nights, but there's something about the phrase you don't feel quite comfortable with. "Well," you say, finally, "they can't help it, right?"

"No, no. Of course not." Adding, after a moment: "Mine were the same."

Somewhere, the bird cries out, louder than ever. "What *is* that?" you ask her, before you can stop yourself, only to watch Mrs Cambres cock her head even further, as though her neck's too stiff to move any other way—just turn and keep on turning, 'til her hidden ear almost brushes her shoulder. "Just a night-bird," she says, her great eyes umber-tinted in the fading light. "There's a story we tell about it, a silly story. Right, *criancas*? The bird that looks for his mother."

"She says they're witches, those birds," Aaron corrects, sleepily, later on, as you tuck him in. "All of them. And that's not what they're looking for, either."

"Witches don't have mommies," Misa argues, from the other side of the bed.

"No, stupid: they *are* mommies, that's what Mrs Cambres said. They're looking for kids, to eat."

"*Their* kids?"

"No, 'cause they don't have any, not anymore. 'Cause they ate *them* all first."

You frown. "Go to sleep," you tell him—both of them. And close the door behind you, leaving it open just a crack.

In the living room, there's that book you forgot to take back to the library, the one you found in your bag the day you finally walked away from Levi—right at the bottom, in a tangle of diapers and snack-packs, when you turned it out on the bed they assigned you at the shelter. The spine is cracked, so every time you open it up it falls to almost this exact line: *Half gods are worshipped in wine and flowers. Real gods require blood.*

That same phrase, over and over. And that same bird outside your window, somewhere in the dark, screaming.

Little Portugal is littler now than it's ever been. Go north, it turns into Korea-town; go south and it's a mess of newcomer territories, all Ethiopian restaurants, Belorussian dry cleaners, Nigerian thrift shops. This is the heart of the old neighbourhood, a nest of stores, garages, churches and houses whose facades don't look like they've changed since either the 1980s, or even the 1950s. Time stands still. Even the payphones aren't digital.

"The *bruxsa*, right, Ma?" Joao calls back to Mrs Abreu, after you somehow let slip what Aaron said, last night. "They turn into—owls, or ravens, or something. Big black birds, only come out at night."

Mrs Abreu doesn't nod, just turns to you, lips frown-pursed. "Who's been telling you about that?" she demands.

"Uh...Mrs Cambres, and it wasn't me, it was my kids."

"Belinha, hey? Well, I wonder. That's a bad story for bed-time; she knows better."

You shrug, helpless; Mrs Abreu keeps on staring, while you busy yourself with cutting chops. And a half-minute later the bell rings as another customer enters, distracting her.

Around hand-over time, meanwhile, Joao tries to coax you into meeting him for a drink at some local place—not for the first time, and probably not the last. He seems like a good guy, big but gentle, but all you can ever think of is how your body betrayed you last time, giving you thoughts like these—Levi seemed nice too, after all, at least by comparison. Because that's how men like him work, you've learned since: find someone who's already isolated, someone with no real sense of what "normal" is, and keep on deforming her standards until there's no firm place anymore, 'til she's left with nothing but the same set of victim's instincts already keeping them alone, and ignorant, and scared.

Get her pregnant, twice, so close together it's like she had twins; allow her to bond with the kids before going back on the attack, so her own biology makes her love them just fiercely enough to fear for them, instead of herself. 'Til everything is a swamp of fear and panic, panic and fear and dread.

What a mistake you were! your mother used to say, between rants—tell you how you'd ruined her, in gory detail, before running your father off and condemning the two of you to that crap-hole you grew up in, an ever-narrowing passage through which you could occasionally glimpse hints of what looked like a better class of people living a better sort of life, something you might aspire to one day, if you could only stay quiet, and pleasant, and clean.

Which only set you up for Levi, in the end—a mistake too, just like Aaron, and Misa. Mistakes, compounded. Mistakes making mistakes, and so on, into infinity.

So no, you're not going out with Joao, not now, not ever: you don't want risk, and you're not scared to admit it. *No one wants a girl with baggage,* that was another of your mother's lines, and ever since Aaron was born, you've felt as though everything inside you keeps shifting around, opening new wounds when the first ones—the worst, the most-lasting—aren't even halfway healed yet. Even your period fluctuates, when it used to be so regular you could tell time by it: comes on a different day each month, often without warning, so hard and fast it's cost you clothes. You don't feel yourself, haven't for years. Like...somebody else. Some*thing* else.

When you get home, Aaron runs to meet you with something in his hand. "Look, Mom," he says. "We found it outside."

"It's *gross,*" Misa adds, brightly.

A nugget of some kind—mud, close-packed. Broken open, it yields dust, grass, compacted mulch and a handful of other, smellier things: broken bones, hollow, sparrow-sized; a beaked skull, crushed flat and twisted, as though forced through some narrow, flexing tube. And something else, at the very bottom: moon-shaped, rimmed in faint glitter, snapped across the bed. Is that...

(a fingernail?)

"From an owl," Mrs Cambres says, over your shoulder. "Hey, Aaron? They swallow things whole, digest what they can, then cough out the rest."

"That's what Miss Saba said—she showed us, in a book. *101 True Facts About Birds of Prey.* Can we get pizza, Mom?"

"Not tonight, honey."

"Daddy'd get pizza," Misa mutters, downcast. She can barely remember Levi, though, hopefully. A few more months, and she'll have lived half her entire life without him in it.

Mrs Cambres has a roof garden, shaded from the sun by a trellis heavy with purple grapes whose bitter skins slip off whole in your mouth when you bite them, insides popping nude and sweet, like eyeballs. She makes her own wine, too, and when she offers you a glass, you take it. Sip it slowly, staring down at the streets you walked to get here from above, while she gives you all the latest gossip about people you barely know, a lulling tangle of equally forgettable names, dates, relationships. It's like having the TV on low, listening to soap operas spool out without knowing any of the particulars, only that the world is full of people at least as unhappy as you've ever been, their choices just as haphazard, as badly-conceived, as ultimately unfulfilling.

"You look tired, *doce,*" Mrs Cambres says, topping you up. "Not sleeping well, hey? Children eat up everything, I know—the worry, the expense. And thinking of him, still, maybe?"

"I...hadn't been," you say, washing the lie down with a swig.

"Might be he looks for you, I suppose. You came some ways, to get here... walked in, Miss Sada says, with just those two and your own shoes, the clothes on your back. That must have been hard."

"Took a while," you agree. "Hours. But at least I had the stroller."

"At least that, yes. Another glass?"

"...please."

That night you dream, for the first time in weeks. You stand on the roof, under the trellis, looking down, and you see Levi pass below you—only from above, obviously, but you know it's him, you know. That hair. That walk. Stamping down the road, hands fisted, eyes roaming: looking for you, for Misa, for Aaron. Looking for trouble, ready to make some, always. Ready to make even more mistakes.

This is my place now, you think. *Mine, not yours. Never yours.*

And you stretch out your arms, black feathers blooming everywhere, wings breaking from your shoulders with a snap, like pirate sails. Eyes rounding, fixing. Fingers and toes sharpening, hooking like great horn blades, serrated raptor's claws.

Look up, you think. *See me, for once. For the very last time.*
Here I am.

"Was a guy in here looking for you, after you left," Joao tells you the next morning, as you let yourself in through the back. He's never waiting for you when you arrive, so you already know something's wrong; Mrs Abreu's opened up early, standing where you usually do, wrapping a rack of ribs. "I didn't tell him anything—didn't think it was my place. But I told Ma, and she said to catch you before you started working."

The ground beneath you seems to heave, up and down, a caught breath. "What did he look like?" you make yourself ask, finally.

"Oh, you know: white guy, 'bout my age. Said his wife ran off, took his kids, he was checking shelters, already got the run-around from Miss Saba. Asked me if I'd seen somebody fit her description."

"That could be anybody."

"Showed me a picture, Sarah; you, and the little ones. Pretty sure it's him."

You want to shut your eyes, but the lids won't cooperate. "I don't know what to do," you say, finally.

Joao shrugs. "Go back to Mrs Cambres's, hole up for a while. We'll keep on stalling him 'til he gets fed up and goes away, then call you when it's safe."

"He's a...he *can* be a very patient man, Joao. When he thinks it matters."

"Yeah, well, what's he gonna do? He calls the cops 'round here, first one turns up's gonna be my uncle, or my cousin. Not to mention if he tries anything else, Ma'll hit him with her broom."

"Thank you. Thank Mrs Abreu for me, too. I—" Now your eyes are filling up, making you blink. "I don't deserve this, you being so understanding. Especially when it's busy."

"Don't be dumb. Now get goin', okay?"

"...okay."

Back out in the alley, the dregs of a hangover make you squint, turning the familiar strange. Everything seemed so pleasant when you walked over, humming, remembering Misa and Aaron in front of their cartoons. Now you almost can't remember the direction you came from, afraid that whichever way you turn, you'll see Levi's face coming around the next corner. You almost run the rest of the way, bent and panting, shielding you face with your fingers; Mrs Cambres opens the door as you fumble with the keys, pulling you in by one wrist—her long nails denting the skin, one degree of micro-pressure away from a scratch—and bolting it behind you.

"Upstairs," she orders. "You need to lie down and gather yourself so you don't frighten the children, looking like that."

"Levi—"

She flourishes a finger in your face, making a scolding sound. "Ch-ch-ch! None of him. No one comes in this house I don't invite them, believe you me. Calm, *doce*. I'll take care of everything."

Upstairs, you pull the covers up to your chin and stare at the ceiling, watching shadows lengthen as the day ticks on. Aaron and Misa play, but quietly, barely registering on the outskirts of your attention; Mrs Cambres might as well not even be in the house, for all the noise she makes.

You fall asleep sometime between early afternoon and late, waking to blue-orange twilight and the sound of your children whispering to each other in the next room, voices fading in and out. "...Daddy?" Misa seems to say, but Aaron shushes her. Then nothing but your own breathing, the steady beat of your heart, trees brushing against the window—and are those footsteps, up above? Mrs Cambres on the roof, tending to her garden?

That bird cries again, closer than ever, making you jump. Like it's in the room with you.

We can't stay inside forever, your mind tells you, weakly. *What if the kids get sick, if they need medicine? What if he comes back, with friends? What if someone else tells him this is where we live? If he can't have me, you know he'll take them, just for spite. And not even because he really wants them, but just because he knows how much it'd hurt—*

When did he become so huge in your mind, exactly? When did he burn that hole in the middle of everything, the one you constantly orbit, through which the light drains out?

When you figured out that the only place left to go for free was the library, you started spending almost the whole day there, after your chores were done. That stopped when you forgot the time, and Levi came looking. He broke your nose in the children's section, and when you wouldn't let them call the cops, they told you both to leave.

A week later you came back, heart beating hard, barely able to breathe— Misa and Aaron both dozing in their big double stroller, the last thing Levi's parents bought for you. You Googled shelters, found the one that looked farthest away, printed out a map, and walked there. It took eight hours, the last three with Misa screaming, Aaron begging you to go back home. But when you got there Miss Sada took you in, and things began to change.

You took nothing with you, or good as. Levi'd made sure there was never anything left around for you to take. No phone. No money. Everything you have now you've made for yourself, aside from whatever came out of the bluff, curt kindness of women like Mrs Abreu, Mrs Cambres—those dark-scarved neighbourhood ladies at the meat-shop, at the dollar store, in the playground-park just outside the church, always sitting there together, waving friendly as the priest walks by, though they never seem to actually go inside. They smile at each other, when they think you can't see; stare up over the rims of their spectacles, fierce front-facing eyes squinting only slightly, peering past you as they speak, always on the look-out for something. Like birds after prey.

A few months ago, when Aaron gave Misa his cold, Mrs Cambres made them cordial you only gave them a few sips of, and only the once. It made them sweat and shiver, complaining about bad dreams. You swallowed some yourself, then poured the rest surreptitiously down the drain, scrubbing the sink out with your fingers. And that night you dreamt you were riding a bicycle down a long, dark hill, straight into the wind until your coat lifted up on either side, tails flapping like wings.

Men aren't worth much, one of Mrs Cambres's cronies once told you, comfortingly—you can't remember her name now, if you were ever told it. *We all know this, hey? You like them, but they don't like you, not really— none of us. That's just how it is.*

Men knock you down, another agreed. *Women lift you up, or should—if they know what's good for them. We'd do away with men entirely, maybe, if they weren't so much fun.*

Hmm, yes, Mrs Cambres put in, fingers busy with her needlework. *Though they do make good eating, sometimes.*

Like children, the second woman replied. And laughed.

Then, all at once, you're suddenly awake, bladder full, mind fear-pricked. You creep into the children's room and stand there looking down at them for what feels like ten minutes, watching them sleep, and wondering: how much of Levi is inside them, deep down? Will Aaron, the sweetest boy you've ever known, one day whisper to a weeping woman that he'd rather see her dead than live without her? Will Misa reckon her love by bruises? Not if you can help it. But can you? Can you really "help" anything?

Never have before, that voice—your mother's voice—whispers in one ear, too fast for you to shake it away, like a mosquito. And you feel a shock run right through you, a bolt to the back of the head, some slaughterhouse kiss: paralyzingly familiar, potentially inevitable.

What if nothing ever does change, really—not permanently, anyhow? Because of weakness, inertia, karma. Because that's just what you deserve. What if—

Enough, another voice replies, possibly out loud, though since the kids don't stir, you're not quite sure. *Come downstairs,* doce. *See what I've done for you.*

You come down slowly, one step at a time. And even from here you can see there's somebody sitting at the kitchen table, hunched forwards with hands folded, his face a blank black blur under the centre-set light. Even from here, by the very way he sits, you can see that it's Levi.

Mrs Cambres sits in front of him, her back to the stairs, to you. So small she barely comes up to his chest. She doesn't look around, not even when— before you can think of stopping yourself—you make a noise like that one bird, high and harsh: all rage, no fear. A hunting owl, about to swoop.

I'll kill him, you think. *He'll never touch them. I'll kill him right here, right now.*

"Oh, no need, *doce,*" Mrs Cambres says, in her creaky voice. "Come closer, and I'll show you."

As you stand there trembling, caught between movements, her head begins to turn, then keeps on turning. Turns until you can hear the pop of cartilage and see both her fierce orange-tinted eyes staring straight into your own, her mouth smiling secretive under that bladed nose, even as her clawed fingers tighten on the table in front of her, carving delicate little runnels into its dark-stained surface. And over her head, you feel your own gaze suddenly sharpen, zooming like a telescope to show you Levi slumped upright in rigour, collar peeled down to reveal that beak-hole knocked straight through his jugular vein, the lapel below soaked black along its edge. How the waxy pallor of his face and hands demonstrates exactly how much blood he's lost, if not where most of it actually *went,* aside from the slopped overflow.

Mrs Cambres licks her lips, one two, mordantly deliberate. One fixed eye twitches, attempting a wink. "*Bruxsa*," you name her, automatically. And see her hands rise, to clap.

"I knew you paid attention," she says, approvingly. And lets her head snap back to where it should be, front-facing, before kicking back her chair and getting up, with a slight *huff* of effort. Muttering, as she does: "Not as young as I was, but well enough still, when there's work to be done. Now, shall we?"

"...shall we what?"

"Go up, *doce*. Let me show you the world, like Satan did for Jesus."

Another blink—yours, this time. After which the two of you stand under her trellis, looking out on the empty street below: black trees, street-lamps burning yellow, casting more shadow than light. Above the sky hangs heavy, no stars, only clouds. Though you don't know what there is to see by, you find you can see just fine, nevertheless: the roof, the garden, her. Yourself.

Hands crooking, nails itching, longing to grow and hook. Back hunching, shoulders flaring, blades sharp as wing-roots. Hair lifting to flare against the moist night wind, a ruff of long, limp feathers.

"So now we come to it," Mrs Cambres tells you. "Your decision, *doce*— to take this gift, or throw it away, unopened? For myself, it was enough to drink that *cahorro* dry, to do what you thought you couldn't...but then, I like you. I always wanted a daughter."

"So—it's all true, then? Witches like birds, drinking blood?"

She makes a little flourish with one hand, dismissive, yet not entirely un-proud. "As you see. We were in Rome and Greece, long before this, meeting at the crossroads, making our prayers to the Three-Faced One, who answers all women. I had a husband, once, fit for nothing but to leave me his name, his house. And children, too—I told you so, hey? How I remembered."

"Yes, you did. What happened?"

"*I* happened. This is the price, *doce*. It's not like God the Father and His soft son. When pain becomes unbearable, we call out to whatever will answer us, and pay with whatever they ask for."

"Aaron...Misa? No, I won't. Never that."

"Then you won't. You don't have to, sweet girl—not yourself, not directly. Not so long as you have me to look after you."

That shock again, straight through the heart, like a nail. "You...stay away from them," you manage, at last. "I'll kill you, you understand? If you even *try*—"

"Like you should have killed *him*, to save us both the trouble? He went to sleep every night, *doce*, right in the same bed; anyone could do it, if they had the will. So *easy*. But you ran instead, hey?" She pauses, owl-eyes flat, pupils narrowing. "Where will you run to now, I wonder?"

Where indeed.

"Nowhere," you say, lashing out, prompted by movement you can't see: that *stoop* before lift-off, a change considered, not yet embarked on. And you push her headlong off the roof before she can even think to take flight, come tapping at your children's window in disguise with sharp beak open, blood-seeking—

—Mrs Cambres, this poor old lady, your only friend, your protector. Her dark scarf ripped free as she falls, too shocked to cry out, scarring the sky.

Mistake, it's a mistake, like always, like everything else: oh, you crazy damn bitch. Why would you do that, *why*?

Because I had to, you think. *Because she killed Levi. Because*—

(—he was *mine* to kill, not hers. And she knew it.)

What if she changes when she hits the ground, though, or before? that voice asks—maybe your mother, maybe yourself—from deep inside. *Who'll stop her then? Didn't think of that, did you?*

No. But it doesn't matter.

I'll stop her, you answer it, without hesitation. *Me.* Then repeat, out loud: "*Me.*"

And find, in the very next instant, that you've already thrown yourself off after her, without a second thought—impossible to stop, this final choice, as perhaps it always was. Taking flight, in flashes: here, there, gone.

Screaming that same lost bird's cry as you plunge, headlong, into the night.

LEO NORMAN

The forest is a confusion of shapes; black forms against a blacker sky. Lightning flashes and, for a fraction of a second, I can see the mud and the trees and the tiny shape of a boy. Then the darkness returns, swallowing him up. The hard rain lances down, slashing my face with icy pellets.

I run on. Every step takes me deeper into the black belly of the forest, further from home. My feet slip on churning mud, catching on secret roots. Again and again I fall. Clawed branches and malicious briars catch at my face and hands. Blood weeps from a thousand tiny lacerations, but I feel nothing.

My husband and my family told me to stay away from this place, but he is hiding, and I must seek.

Giant sycamores sway wildly as I pass. Strange mushrooms and fungi lurch and leer from the shelter of silvery trunks. In the distance, over the hiss of the rain, over the wind and the thunder, I hear him calling.

Mummy!

The rolling, roiling clouds part, revealing a slender quadrant of moon. I see the mossy green of a hill to my left, impenetrable gorse to my right. The forest wants me to go on. This way. This way.

And then my foot finds nothing but air and I am falling, then sliding, then tumbling down into the valley of a river. My head strikes the bank and the world flashes white, purple, green. The stars dance. I skid to a stop and lie panting, half buried in mud.

Time passes and the tears come again. My pajamas are torn and my skin is a mess of wounds. Hair sticks to my face like strands of congealed blood.

STICKS AND BONES

Mummy!

His voice echoes deep in the woods and deep in my mind. I try to call out but my voice is swallowed up by great, empty sobs.

I try to rise, but my trembling arms collapse and my face sinks into the mud. I panic. I can't breathe. When I come up, spluttering in the almost-light, I see a flicker of movement on the far bank. I blink away mud, clawing at my face with my hands, but when I look again, there is nothing there.

Something seems familiar about this place. I've scoured these woods a hundred times and know every nook, every crevice – but this feeling is different. It tingles in my gut.

I picture a small child splashing through the stream, laughing. When he clambers over the crest of the bank, he turns back, waving for me to follow.

Desperate, I try once more to clamber to my feet, but the ground is treacherous and I stumble back to my knees.

The voice is still calling. Slowly, I realize what it is he wants me to do.

I clench my fists and scrabble about in the mud. There. I see it. I hold them. Sticks, some pebbles, more sticks, mud, lots of mud. I gather them up, press them together into a small sticky ball. Tears, mud, rain and blood wash from my face and arms, then trickle down across my creation.

I widen my search, crawling across the sloppy bank, thrusting armfuls of reeds and fistfuls of dead leaves into the mess. More sticks follow, held together by more mud, more blood, more tears.

Lightning flashes again and the sky rumbles. The storm is upon me. On the other bank, exposed by the flash, lies a strange shape, small and misshapen. It calls to me. He wants me to have it.

The river was probably no more than a trickle of stream this morning, before the rains came. Now, swollen like a mother's belly, it fills the little ravine. Water roars and thrashes along its restless bed.

The thing I have made is a mess of oozing parts, but I know I need it. I cannot let it go. Not this time. Instead, I hold the muddy mass above my head and wade in.

Cold slaps my legs, driving icy needles into my calves. What little energy remains in my battered body is sucked away on the surging current and I stumble. I grit my chattering teeth and press on. The ground beneath the water is hard and small rocks cut my feet. Driven on, I struggle through the water and collapse to my knees on the other side of the river.

Here it is. We are face to face. We look at each other with mutual understanding. I know you. You know me. I reach down and the head gives way. It creaks and groans.

The rotted carcass of a fawn, all bones and frothy, molten flesh.

"Come to me, little baby, don't you cry." My words are hushed. I know that somewhere, out there in the dark, its mother is grieving.

I find a sheltered spot on the ground nearby and put down my bundle. When I turn back, the fawn's head twists in the wind and its broken lower jaw droops in a lunatic grin.

We'll be good for each other, I know that he needs me. I pick him up and cradle him in my arms.

This is love.

When I grip the mangy fur of his neck, it sags, but won't tear. I pull with all my might. Bones pop. Putrid flesh drips on my knees. But no luck.

"Please, my love. Come to me."

I take the pelt between my teeth and bite. A stench of sweetness and rot fills my nose and I gag. The body squelches beneath my touch. I bite harder and slip my hand through a hole in its flesh. When I pull, it sounds like tearing Velcro.

I feel tendons snap and meat slide from the bone. I feel as the creature's spine slides out from under the flesh and the head comes loose.

I hold it aloft. Lightning flashes and I see the full, beautiful horror of my love. Devoid of eyes, mouth still grinning, ears pulled back in heightened anticipation, the fawn's head is finally free.

But it's not yet time. He's not complete. I place the head carefully down on the bank, returning my attention to the rest of the corpse.

I begin the slow process of appropriating bones and stinking entrails into my packet of stick and stones. It begins to take shape. I take off my dressing gown and swaddle it in my loving arms.

Finally, I am ready. I lift the head from the bank and place it on top, pressing the fragment of spine deep in its back.

Lightning claps. Thunder roars. The trees sway in their dance; more erratic, more maniacal than ever.

Holding him to my chest, I feel something growing within me. A powerful force is rising up from the depths of my stomach. Air rushes in through my mouth and through my nose. My chest swells. I feel as if I will burst.

I scream.

The sound echoes around the narrow river valley and off into the forest. When it comes back, it has doubled, intertwined with the scream of my boy.

I am out of the guts of the river, holding my son in my arms. His eyes are closed. His breath tickles my neck. The rain has stopped. The wind has calmed. The wrinkled bark of giant oaks glistens in the moonlight.

My child whimpers. His nose is wet and warm.

"It's okay." I squeeze him tighter. "Mummy's here."

But I am lost. The way back is murky. The storm still rages there. I must press on.

I wander deeper into the woods.

The all-knowing oaks give way to denser, taller, pines. Their silver trunks line my path and, high above, their haughty canopies shiver in the breeze. A lone pine cone drops, clattering through high branches, before plopping into the mud.

I crouch to pick it up, rolling it in frozen fingers, then slip it in my pocket.

As I stand, a large, white moth brushes against my ear and I flinch. It jigs about it front of me, like a mad, hairy butterfly.

"Nachtfalter," I murmur. I haven't spoken the language of my childhood for decades. I reach out a hand and the moth lands on my finger. It has tiny white hairs around its head, like a fur coat. "Lead me home."

With a thrust of its wings, the moth takes flight. It bobs before me and zigzags off into the night, lurching up and down like a drunk.

I clutch my son in my arms and follow.

The moth flits from tree to tree, dipping behind bushes and re-emerging further on. The pale moonlight dances on its back as it cavorts in the darkness. When the wind blows, the moth dodges between water droplets and on, on, into he dark.

I plod along behind it, cuddling my baby. Images of another child flash in the depths of my mind and I squeeze my eyes shut, pushing them away. I did this for him.

When I open them, the moth has vanished. Panic grows like the lungs swelling in my chest. The moth made me feel safe.

An owl hoots and I look up to see a large, black silhouette gliding over my head. I break away from the path and follow the dark bird into the woods.

I look at my son and plant a kiss on his long, soft nose. When his eyes open they yawn emptily under the moonlight. I smile. So pretty. And mine.

The owl leads me through a patch of large, mossy ash trees. Their trunks look tired. Their branches are the bony arms of childless mothers. They weep leaves as I pass.

The ground is no longer muddy but spongy. With each step, I sink deeper into the marsh. Soon I am wading up to my knees in freezing water. Mud sucks at my feet. It doesn't matter, I have to keep going. Something warm throbs in my pocket.

The owl swoops overhead. It knows where we're going.

With simple, silent elegance, the owl lands on the hooked arm of an ash. His head rotates left and right, scouting our next way. Then it looks right at me. Its eyes are black and lifeless. It holds the crumpled wings of a moth in its hard beak.

I freeze.

Where is he leading me?

The forest gets stranger with every step. Huge, bushy ferns sprout from the ground, and the water is rising. Large red half-moons of fungi scale the trees. The wind is rising, singing a song of loss, moaning words from the past: errinnern.

It is getting harder to move. Icy water comes up to my waist, sucking me down. I hold my precious bundle aloft, desperate to continue, but I can't carry on. My fingers are blue. My legs are numb.

My arms sag. I feel the weight of the sticks and the bones in my bundle of rags. Sticks and bones. Death.

What have I done?

I stagger up onto a mossy mound and lean against a tree. My eyes droop shut. My breathing slows.

The heat in my pocket pulses through my side.

This is the end. I will die here, alone, in the forest my son loved to run and play in. I will never find him, not even his corpse.

The bundle drops from my arms. I feel it spill to the floor with a splash.

With limp arms, I pull the pine cone from my pocket. It is soft and warm. It throbs in my palm. With a last, feeble effort, I push it into the chest of my earthen child.

Darkness is creeping in. The cold is leaving me.

Something taps on my shoulder.

I open one blurred, spasming eye.

A boy stands before me with the face of a deer.

"Mummy" he whispers.

I try to reach out, but I'm too weak. I can't reach him.

Instead, he reaches me. A tiny, delicate hand slips into mine. It's warm.

The life that had drained from my body comes flooding back.

"Mummy, come with me." The voice is Tommy's – my son's.

I feel at peace. The wind has stopped blowing. The air is still.

Tommy smiles at me through his long, hairy jaw, then leads me gently out of the forest.

A Marvelous Neutrality

ESTHER SAXEY

A poet had invited my husband and I to dinner.

"Must it be tonight, Mehmet? It's such short notice."

"He sent me a message at the Museum! He wishes to talk about angels."

We had been living in London for a only week, but I had glimpsed a hundred differences between Egyptian and English manners. "I thought we might dine with your colleagues first."

"Amina, my dear, surely good manners matter less than good intentions? And his grandfather is a Duke!"

In the hansom cab, I tried to bring to mind what I knew of angels. They are made of light. They sit high up in the articles of faith, coming after Allah (of course), but before His books, His messengers, and the day of judgement. Our carriage's jolting progress over the cobbles summoned up names: Jibrael, Mikael, Israfil, Malik.

I knew I was being unfairly jealous. Mehmet and I had spent every day together on the ship to England, and now he worked while I read guide books and wandered department stores with our maid. I needed to share my husband with the world, for his happiness—and my own. How many other women had such opportunities?

We climbed out of the cab, and up the stone stairs of a great townhouse. My husband tapped on the door.

"Mehmet, love, I've not read any of his poetry! What is it about?"

"He wrote a wonderful verse-story about an unjust king. It's a little like *The Eloquent Peasant*."

"Good! What else?"

"Oh, he wouldn't expect you to have read his recent poems. They are rather improper."

My stomach sunk. "Then how can it be proper for me to dine with him, Mehmet?"

His face crumpled because my sharp words had broken his unworldly heart and the door swung open before I could make amends.

The poet's footman seemed loath to step out of the dark hallway. He leaned his long body around the doorframe and his head weaved as examined us. Copper stubble glinted along his pale jaw.

"Mehmet, my good fellow!" He reached out a hand to clap my husband on the shoulder but missed.

It was not the footman but the Poet himself.

"So, Mehmet. You've committed to our endeavour. I thought you were going to disappoint me."

"Not at all! May I introduce my—"

"You and I will speak with angels."

"I would be very glad to speak *of* angels. But I fear I—"

"Too modest, my friend! We will batter on the very gates of Heaven. Did you bring the necessary things?" He coiled an arm around my husband's shoulders and started to drag him away. I coughed.

The Poet spun to face me. "Mehmet, you've cheated. You've brought your own angel with you. Not allowed at all."

Was that gallantry? It held no hint of welcome. My husband and I shared a weak smile. At least our manners would not be the worst at dinner.

The drawing room he led us to smelled musky, as though a fox had rubbed itself through the clutter. The curtains were drawn, and by the gaslight I saw such glorious things. Benin bronzes, brass Tibetan singing bowls, painted ostrich eggs, all crammed onto shelves and spilling onto the floor. I was dazzled, then distressed. Chosen for their rarity, these treasures were jumbled into a squalid existence.

A short old man with a beard neat as a brush stood among them.

"This is Professor Quixano," the poet said. "You must get along well. Very friendly, no fighting. We're all people of the Book." He smirked and hurried my husband into the next room. Mehmet carried the small suitcase he'd brought with him. I suspected it was full of books to consult and lend.

"I lecture in Hebrew at the University College," said the professor.

"Pleased to make your acquaintance. Is your wife joining us?"

"I'm not married. Not yet!"

So I would be the only woman at dinner—improper, again. Although it was the poet's fault, it made me self-conscious. I looked to the windows, as if I could summon a breeze. The curtains glittered, beaded borders brushing the carpets. I recognised them as Indian sarees. For a moment I had the unpleasant notion that the Poet had stripped them off women.

"Mrs Basha? What is your husband's field?"

"He studies inscriptions. On tiles, at the moment."

"And are they pretty?"

"They are naskh and kufic script," I said, so that he would not condescend to me all evening.

Blessedly, he laughed. "Forgive me, An honest question, my own texts are often deathly dull to look at! You're from Egypt? It must be nearly as hot here, at the moment."

"Almost." But England seemed badly prepared for such temperatures, by comparison. The buildings were sweltering and the parks had shrivelled. The clothes I'd purchased at Liberty,summer dresses they assured me, were tight-fitting and heavy.

"May I get you something for your thirst?" He held out a decanter. I wondered how the poet had mislaid his household staff.

"Is there anything but wine?" The professor shook his head. I accepted a small glass to moisten my mouth. My father drank sometimes, when we had European visitors. The wine tasted vinegary.

"Our host must be delighted to have found your husband."

"How do you mean?" I had thought my husband more eager than his host.

"Our host asked me here to look at some writing in an unknown alphabet. He has certain books, by Dr Dee." He said the name with glee and it rang like struck brass. "He asked me whether the writing related to Hebrew."

"And does it?"

"Complete gibberish, as far as I could see. Now, your husband is probably my counterpart. I imagine our host is showing him the same writing, to see if it's Arabic. And if it is, all the secrets of the Heavens will be unlocked for our young poet!"

"Goodness."

"So, the question is: how quickly can your husband deliver bad news? I'd like to dine before nine."

I knew Mehmet would be in agonies at disappointing our host.

Professor Quixano misinterpreted my pained look. "I promise we won't talk business over dinner. But this Dr Dee is an interesting chap, very interesting. Do you know anything about him?"

I offered something that Mehmet had told me. "Did he speak to angels?"

The Professor's eyes twinkled.

"What a question! Did he, indeed. Dee was a sort of court conjurer for Queen Elizabeth; horoscopes and alchemy, three hundred years ago. And he spoke to angels, maybe." Professor Quixano frowned. "Our host wishes to write a poem about Dee's talks with angels."

"Do you study angels?" The room's air was opressive and pressed me from different directions as if I sat in a slow-swirling current. I drank more, hoping to feel better.

"No, but I'm interested in the messages they can carry. Dee's angels spoke a language which was shared by all people, so they said. And they told Dee to share all his goods with his friend, Kelley. Now, our poet host," The professor rolled his eyes, "he's very fashionable. What if he wrote a poem about how the angels *tell us to share*? Regardless of nation, or religion? If he wrote such a thing, and did it well, I wouldn't think this evening a waste."

I couldn't hide my pessimism. "Could our host carry such a message?"

"Certainly, certainly! He's a rich man himself, of course, but that's an advantage, When a poor man speaks of fair shares, they call it sour grapes. And he wrote that doggerel about the tyrant king, which was half-way to Republicanism."

"But his reputation..."

Professor Quixano dismissed my doubts with a wave of his hand. "His nasty poems were only published in France. Most people haven't heard of them. They're piffling and ridiculous"

Just then, the poet returned.

My husband trailed after him, most apologetic. "Of course, if I could take a sample, or a copy, I could make more thorough checks..."

The mysterious writing had obviously proved not to be Arabic.

The poet clicked his fingers impatiently. "Come along, people of the book. Get into that room, we need to prepare. Fear not. Hurry-scurry."

I'd hoped for food. I felt bad from drinking, but the darkened room we entered was not a dining room.

Desks on either side held huge open books covered in a strange cramped script, lines slanting across pages, forming boxes and columns and stars. This was the script which was not Hebrew, and not Arabic. Peering at it frustrated me, this language that was supposedly shared by all people but which nobody could read.

"Make yourselves useful and light those," said the poet, pointing at a dozen candles set around the books and tossing the professor a box of matches.

My husband and the professor lit candles together. I heard the professor suggest they should meet later that month and perhaps increase the connections between Museum and University. I was glad some good would come out of the evening. To allow them to talk more, I moved further off.

At the head of the room stood a table covered with black velvet. Resting on the velvet were purple quartz crystals as large as my head, and between them, paintings—icons, small, but with beetle-bright colours.

I saw the paintings were all of angels.

They each were portrayed with a flimsy pair of dove-like wings. It seemed to me they would need wings both stronger and more numerous. Jibrael was described as having hundreds of wings. To come to earth from heaven couldn't be an easy flight.

"So very vivid," murmured the poet into my ear. "And do you have angels where you come from?"

All four of us held some angels in common, I was certain of it: Jibrael became Gabriel, Mikael was Michael. The poet's ignorance annoyed me. "Oh, yes. Dozens. Should I have brought some with me?"

The poet scowled. "Well, your husband has provided something useful, at least."

My husband's small suitcase lay open on the floor. The poet stooped and lifted a small bundle of fabric from it. For a moment, it seemed as though he reverently held a crumpled sock.

He unwrapped a bright crystal sphere as big as a hen's egg.

"Dr Dee's shewstone!"

And from the suitcase, again, another object: this one round, black, perfectly polished, and about the size of his face.

"And his obsidian mirror. Now we'll see something for sure."

Light slid across the surface of the mirror as he placed both objects on the velvet table top.

My husband had brought these things with him in his suitcase, but neither object was ours. They hadn't come with us from Cairo. Where had he found them? I'd shopped in London, but he'd been busy working.

"You didn't bring the Seal of God," the poet said.

"I am sorry, it is made of wax, and is too easily damaged. And I must take everything back tonight, of course."

Despite the heat, my skin turned cold. My husband had stolen the things from the museum.

"Let us all pray that the mysteries shall be known to us!" said the poet.

I wanted to snatch up the objects and my husband, and drag them home. How could he risk his job and treat a National Museum like a circulating library? Was he dazed by the prospect of meeting a poet-aristocrat, who was nothing more than a shabby man in a stinking house?

I watched the poet stroke the stolen black mirror, muttering to himself. "Angel of the seven-pointed star, show to us knowledge of all metals! Come forth, Madimi!"

I couldn't bear this charlatan taking a share of my husband's admiration.

"I feel unwell," I said, loudly. My head ached. But I also hoped my beloved would take me aside, or even outdoors, where we could speak privately. It was not too late to leave.

"You're hungry," the Poet said, laying the mirror aside. "We should all eat. I have a cold collation, quite equal to the occasion."

My husband's eyes met mine. My clever husband, who had studied at Al-Azhar, was begging me to dine with a drunkard.

But a wealthy drunkard and perhaps an influential one. I reminded myself of all I had gained from Mehmet's curiosity and enthusiasm. My Father was kind and wealthy, but I would never have seen London without Mehmet.

And the theft was done and, I prayed, undiscovered. Little would be gained from leaving early.

We would stay. And if we were staying, we should eat, to face the evening as calmly as we could. So I nodded to Mehmet and we followed the poet out of the weird dark chamber and through the drawing room, into a far brighter space where a dining table was laid.

I had feared the food might be insanitary, but it looked deliciously fresh. The cutlery shone. The tablecloth was spotless, apart from a plump bee resting on one corner. Windows were open onto a garden and birdsong poured in.

Why then, did the sight of it unnerve me?

Because the meal had taken more than one person to prepare it, but it wouldn't need a soul to serve it.

Our host had chosen this meal so he could send his servants away for the evening.

I began by taking a little of every dish, for the sake of politeness, then realised nobody cared if I was slighting the hard-boiled-egg salad in favour of the roast chicken. I could have eaten better if not for the bees. At my request the windows were closed, but it was impossible to rid the room of them. They droned past my face, blundering against my eyes and lips.

The men talked of angels.

"Why did the angels speak to Dee, in particular?" asked Professor Quixano.

"They didn't," the poet explained. "His friend Kelley was the scryer, Kelley heard the angels. Dee wasn't sensitive enough. The angels won't speak to just anyone."

"And I suppose you're hoping you'll be a scryer, yourself?" asked the professor. "You being so sensitive."

The poet, immune to mockery, spread out his hand as if to say, *who else*?

Then he jumped, startled by a sharp crack against the window pane. A bee had banged against the glass, and now wavered away.

Beware of wavering, I thought, and then wondered why.

"One of the angels told Kelley, 'I am Prince of the Seas: I drowned Pharoah.'" The poet sat back, satisfied, as though he had submerged Pharoah himself.

I thought of the waters rolling back over Pharoah's army. Rushing into the gap with relief, like a breath held for too long and then let go, making the surface smooth again.

My husband looked nauseated at the mention of drowning. He'd been seasick on the voyage here. To distract him, I asked the professor to retell his story about the egalitarian angels.

Professor Quixano did so, with relish and embellishments, and my husband smiled wanly.

"How interesting! That sounds very..." He mulled over the correct word.

"Amiable?" said Professor Quixano.

"Amicable," said my husband.

"Animal," I said.

"I beg your pardon, my darling?"

"Amicable, as you said. A very friendly notion."

But for some reason, I had ceased to see sharing as a virtue. A hive shares all things. Does that make it virtuous? I thought of a bee angel, furred limbs in robes, wings not like a dove but made of veined glass. I swatted the angelbee away from my thoughts. Was the buzzing coming from inside my head now? It was too dense in my head, too airy outside. I needed to get what was in my head out, to equalise the pressure. I had a sudden joyful vision of piercing my skull with a fork.

"Amina, my dear." Mehmet had placed a morsel of his own food onto my plate to tempt me. A bee landed on it. Yet he still looked expectant.

"I can't eat that."

I saw my confusion mirrored in his face.

I looked down at my cutlery. In the bowl of my spoon, a dark shape was moving—not a bee, but a reflection. It slid around the top of the spoon, changing form: tall, then squat, then willowy again. It was a girl-child, walking across the room behind me.

A maid, come to clear the dinner? But the maids weren't home, and even in the indistinct and sliding image, she seemed too young to be a maid. Perhaps some relative of the poet, although who would trust him with their child?

Her feet made no sound, or maybe she was inaudible above the buzzing of the bees, the bees whose numbers were still increasing. They came from the other rooms. They came from the same place as the girl.

I stopped myself from turning my head to see where she could not be.

She whispered to me. "I will teach thee names without numbers."

"I don't want them."

"Perhaps a glass of water?" my husband said.

"Water?" sneered the Poet. He lifted a bottle of champagne and uncorked it, with a sharp pop and a splatter of foaming light.

I babbled excuses and escaped into the hallway, but the poet followed me.

"Did you like my angels? The icons?"

"They're charming." But their wings weren't strong enough.

The pressure in my head, and the pop of the champagne cork, had helped me to understand it. A door is hard to open when the wind is against it;

likewise, for the angels to pass over into our own world there would have to be an evenness on either side. An evenness of what, though? I didn't know. Of air? Of awe? Of everything?

I would not speak of angels to the poet.

"You liked what the professor said about sharing possessions?" His eyes glittered. Had he seen how angry I'd been about the purloined Museum artefacts? Did he mean to justify his theft by heavenly instruction?

I managed some bland words. "It is a sweet thought."

"Sweet as honey." The poet's hand slithered up the outside of my leg. "The angels told Dee and Kelley to share their wives as well."

I took his hand off my leg. I considered taking his hand off his arm as well with the blunt silver cutlery.

"Don't touch me."

"It is an English custom," the poet lied.

"Really? My dear husband is very interested English customs, should I tell him of it?"

The poet fled.

I considered this new angelic instruction. I was quite sure the angels had no interest in the sly fumbling the poet was attempting. If they had truly told Dee and Kelley to share their wives, it was because the couples' fidelity, their specificity, was a kind of tangle. The angel needed to make everything smooth, and everyone become one.

I rejoined the party as the poet announced that we would now speak with the angels. My husband and the professor shrugged and agreed. I saw my chance and excused myself.

My husband hung back behind the other two so he could hold out his hand to me. I squeezed it. It was dry, solid, and warm.

"You aren't unwell, love?"

"I only need some rest." The evening would be over soon and when we were home, I would tell him everything. I would not share my husband with this ridiculous man again.

I sat in the drawing room. Through the closed door I heard them speak in unison but still with distinction between them: the Poet's high-pitched frenzy, Professor Quixano's mumble and my love's voice was fine, almost singing.

On a bookcase I found a volume of the poet's French writings, a cycle of sonnets called *Melusine*: women became snakes, women loved men, women loved women, some of whom were snakes. I could imagine the Poet cranking a handle to produce the tedious series of obscene combinations.

The buzzing in the room—or in my head—sounded more mechanical than organic now. A treadle sewing machine running fast and hard might sound that way, punching a needle endlessly through the air.

I heard the poet shout: "*Pactum factum*!"

I looked up from the book of poems and saw the girl again walking across the room towards me.

Her dark hair floated like pondweed in the sultry air. Her dress was red, then green, then red again. She came to me, picking her way through the clutter on the floor of the room. It was as if the objects moved to allow her to pass.

"Beware of wavering," she said.

I begged her pardon. I begged her mercy. She recoiled at my uncertainty, the unevenness of my purpose.

I felt her attention turning to the men next door, and with her I sensed the poet's arrogance and the professor's amusement. And there with them, my dear husband. His warm desire to please was waning because of his abhorrence of blasphemy. The dips and peaks of his temperament felt sweetly familiar to me.

The angels would smooth away all these things.

I knew the girl was only the tiniest tendril of what was to come. A wisp of smoke curls up from under a door when behind the door, a furnace rages. When the rest arrived, they would not look like her. Jibrael visited Mary in the form of a man, but he was not a man.

They would not have wings, either. They would not beat their wings to carry them through the aethers. They would make every mountain low, raise up every valley, melt the rough places into smoothness. They would make everything even, everything the same, and slide over to our world in an effortless procession.

Share everything, make everything equal; these were not divine messages but practical instructions, as a ship's captain shouts to the harbour crew.

"I will teach thee names without numbers," the girl offered again. She showed me how much the angels yearned to cross over.

I said no.

The buzzing within became a vibration that shook my bones until I thought the flesh would slough from them. I flung my arms around myself and gripped tightly. My teeth rattled.

The girl stood in front of me. She opened her dress. I forced my chin down onto my chest and buried my face in my hands.

"Open your eyes and you shall see from the highest to the lowest."

"I don't want to."

I didn't want them to show me how they would make the highest and the lowest all alike.

I told her without speaking that I didn't want to know them, that I didn't want to speak with angels. That the poet was the one who had called her.

I said, "I cannot bear your messages."

And then, the noise began.

It was a grinding, churning roar coming from the next room. A wave surging over the longest beach in the world, dredging and inverting every pebble was how I heard it. But I understood it, with my mind and my heart, as a ripping apart of particles. It was happening to everything that was densely packed: the oak tables, the old books. All these things were being brutally evened out until they were all of one density with the dusty air.

I prayed. When the fear from not seeing grew worse than the fear of what I might see, I opened my eyes again, and the girl was gone.

I crawled to the door and opened it. How could I not? My love was inside.

Turquoise blue light filled the room. It could have been blinding, but it came from so far away that it was weaker than a Spring morning. And it was fading.

The angels had abandoned their attempt.

Inside the room everything had been made even, utterly shared. Furniture and floorboards had been turned to the consistency of cloudy soup. Larger fragments drifted through this haze like dust motes, shreds of paper, and threads of cloth. Some of them sparkled like grains of quartz crystal, I supposed. The fragments were drifting slowly to the floor.

My husband wasn't there. He had been an unevenness. He had been evened out.

The vibrations slowed to a long throb that ran through me and died away.

I was standing ankle deep in a rising sludge made of everything and everyone in the room.

~

When the inquest is over, I will go back to my father's house in Cairo. I will never again share my husband, or this story, with anyone.

> *A marvellous neutrality have these things mathematical, and also strange participation between things supernatural, immortal, intellectual, simple and indivisible, and things natural, mortal, sensible, compounded and divisible.*
>
> *(John Dee, 1570)*

Plague Mother

JAMIE KILLEN

The young sister waits until the ward is quiet, until all the other nuns have gone to sleep. Once she is sure that she is alone, she slips bedside to the patient she has chosen. It's a young man, one who has begun moaning and plucking at his bedcovers with the last stages of the illness. Mother Superior has seen the signs as well, has shaken her head and quietly told the groundskeeper to prepare a grave in the pest house yard.

The sister moves along the walls, in the shadows, between the narrow beds full of stinking patients, and kneels beside the young man. He is well beyond consciousness. There is no danger that he will stir, even as she makes a slit in his leg with the small knife she keeps in the folds of her habit. She fixes her mouth to the wound and calls the illness. It hears her whisper right away. Strange, but the sister never pictures disease as a vapor or a spirit or any of the other things Father Andrew has said cause it. She pictures it instead as a multitude of tiny creatures, strange wormlike things that attack the flesh like an invading army. They swim faster than his blood flows, swarm down her throat in a bitter wave. She keeps sucking, pulling every last one out of him and deep into her belly.

She leans back and peers at the young man in the dark, dabbing at her mouth. He already looks better, his breathing more steady. Tomorrow he will be nearly recovered, and the other nuns will nod and believe that their prayers worked.

The sister stands, and a cramp seizes her middle. She touches her abdomen, now taut and rounded. It has caught her by surprise this time. Usually it happens every twenty or thirty times, and it has only been five times since the last one.

She slips quietly from the ward and out the back gate, gritting her teeth against another pang. There is a glen in the forest beyond the churchyard, a hidden place she uses for these times. The ferns are soft and cool against her back when she lays down, help distract her from the pain.

It takes only a few minutes of breathing and forcing herself not to cry out when she knows it's time. She hikes up her shift and parts her legs, clenches her teeth with the first hard push.

This is the moment when the sister is always seized by dread, no matter how many times she has done this. It is because she never knows what will come out. They have come in so many different sizes and shapes, skin soft and downy or hard as a turtle shell. She fears that one day there will be one that is too big or too sharp, and that will be the day she dies.

But that day is not yet here. This one comes out easier than most of the others, slides slick and dark onto the damp ferns. She sits up, wincing at the raw throb between her legs. This one has an odd form, all boneless wavy limbs like the body of an eel. It lifts itself shakily onto its hairless legs, totters a few uncertain steps forward.

The ferns rustle around the sister as her other children arrive, creeping from hollows and hidden places. There is Joshua, with his hard ivory skin like sheets of bone, who clatters as he walks. Miriam, made entirely of the finest strands of hair, who flutters in the wind from branch to branch. Twins Michael and Aaron, identical limbless pieces of rust-colored meat studded with different eyes, who must roll from one place to the next. And others still behind them. They all peer through the leaves at their new sibling.

The sister lifts the new one to her breasts, now swollen with the strange black milk that comes with each of the children. She murmurs soothing nonsense as the child latches on and suckles, feels that familiar sadness as she clutches the baby to her body. There will only be this one night, this one feeding. She tried at first to care for them longer, but they always wander off into the trees and fend for themselves after the first night. She has never learned what they do out here, what they eat or where they sleep; the villagers say there are monsters in the woods that steal the young and consume livestock, but the sister is certain they must not mean her children. People must have been telling stories about monsters in the woods long before she came to the pest house, must tell such stories of all dark and quiet forests.

I suppose it's for the best they wander away, she thinks. She knows that the other sisters would not find them beautiful as she does.

The older ones pull close to her, nuzzling her arms and reaching out to welcome their new little sister. Their mother strokes their heads gently, whispers their names, names all chosen from tales of saints or from the Bible. She can remember the plagues that created each of them. Typhoid, the pox, London's Great Pestilence, cholera, influenza. The pest house takes them all, and so does she.

The sister looks down at her youngest. "Cecilia," she whispers. "That will be your name. From Saint Cecilia the Martyr."

She closes her eyes and lets herself enjoy the closeness of her brood. Soon she will have to stand and limp inside and continue the night watch in the ward. Tomorrow will be the time for rest, and if needs be she can plead woman's pains and Mother Superior will give her time to recover. But, for now, she lets herself linger.

It's when she's in the woods like this that the sister finds it hard to remain humble. Even the Blessed Mother only had one Virgin Birth. The sister wonders if God has chosen one of her children in particular, a single messiah, or if they are all angels.

GREENER
PASTURES

MICHAEL WEHUNT

"You ever can't sleep?" the trucker said.

Forsyth glanced up out of his thoughts. The man standing at his table was big and worn out, his eyes raw and heavy even in the shadow of his cap bill. He had a young face with an old beard matted on the left side, as though he'd been trying to nap against the window of his cab.

The trucker slid into the booth. Forsyth didn't answer his question at first. He felt the contradiction of road-life, that of the lonesome loner. It could be nice to have company when he stopped off someplace, but he'd never been much for talk. He glanced around the diner. A couple more long-haulers sat on high stools at the counter, knives and forks chattering against their plates. The waitress was somewhere back in the kitchen. Even for a graveyard shift the place had a tired air.

Forsyth was bleary-eyed himself. Two grinding days, Little Rock to Birmingham to Atlanta and now he was racing the sun to Valdosta. Coming up on three hours of dark left, and by first light he meant to be on the cot in the back of his empty trailer. He'd have enough time for a quick snooze, and then all the state troopers in hell couldn't keep him from his daughter's sixth birthday the next night. Last week the two of them had started reading their first bedtime story together. Lizzie had fallen asleep just as the wolf huffed and puffed at the second pig's house. Forsyth couldn't wait to finish it. He'd been getting along with his ex-wife, too. No way was he losing that momentum.

The big trucker watched him across the booth. "You ever can't sleep?" he asked again.

"I got a feeling," Forsyth told him, "you're not talking about putting off a nap until you get to where you're going."

"No, I'm not." The trucker stared out the window as he spoke.

Forsyth followed his eyes. Only things out there were four rigs lined up in the gloom beyond the sodium lamps and an old Ford wagon off to the far side. Those lamps weren't doing much against the miles of night surrounding the place. Even the lights set into the diner's flat roof didn't seem to touch the lot. Still, it was just another diner along I-75. It didn't have a town around it, that was all.

Forsyth turned back to his temporary buddy. "Insomnia, then? That it?"

"Something like it," the trucker said, and his face reflected in the window seemed...Forsyth didn't want to call it spooked. Distracted, maybe. Enough years spent boxed in on tiresome roads and it was a simple thing to think a man was haunted.

"Hell, I think I've slept about every way a man can," Forsyth said. "I got used to it. How long you been hauling?"

"Three years, nearing on four."

"I get my two-year badge next month. How long you had insomnia?"

He turned and regarded Forsyth with those weary eyes. "I didn't say it was insomnia. I said it was something like it, didn't I?" And his gaze went back out the window.

"That you did, fella." Forsyth wasn't about to whet that edge in the man's voice, but he was curious. "I'm Forsyth, by the way. And before you ask, yes, that's my first name. My mother's maiden name."

He stuck his hand out but the trucker kept on searching the dark, absently turning his coffee mug around on the table. It produced a slow, maddening scrape.

"So what is it, then, if it's not insomnia?" He went back to his hash browns and eggs, left the man to his view.

"You ever wonder if anything's out there with us? When we're driving through the night and all these big gaps of world between towns? You got pieces of map where you can lay a quarter down and there's nothing under it."

"You mean the rural areas?" Forsyth asked.

He waved that aside. "No, no. That's not what I'm saying, man. I don't mean like farms and woods, this road connecting to that road so you can go from there to here. I'm talking about the *space* in between."

"I'm not sure I—"

He cut Forsyth off, really throwing himself into gear now. "I'm curious what it is that makes all that space up. And can it take notice of you. Might be the wondering that draws it. I knew a guy once, this was up in South Dakota, he'd haul loads for miles with just the headlights for company. Black as a pit out there, I can tell you. Not many lights strung along some of those roads. Well, Hitch—we called him that because he'd get bored and pick up hitchhikers—he went missing last year. Cops found his rig idling on a shoulder in the middle of nowhere. Right in one of those pieces of map."

Forsyth pushed his cold eggs away. The trucker stared at his hands for a minute before looking back outside.

"There's something about the lonely places. Something about us folks who go to them. Like rest stops. A month ago I saw Hitch at one in Virginia. Guy was peeking out of the trees behind the bathrooms whispering my name. I could hear him grinning. He started talking about the sky dripping on him, the night folded over like a blanket. He asked me to—oh Jesus."

"What?" Forsyth peered through the glass to see what had put that sudden watery groan in the trucker's last words. It was still just a parking lot, silent and waiting for cars. This place was from a faded era. He doubted it saw many customers even in the best of times. That was half the reason he'd stopped here.

"It's darker," the trucker said. "Look close and you can see everything slinking around."

Forsyth thought he was right about the dark, at least. The streetlights near the entrance, long necks on fifteen-foot stems, were out. The diner huddled in its own small glow now. An island. He could just pick out his rig—a glimpse of red paint—alongside the others, and he could see the edges of the forest that wanted to swallow it all. But nothing moved.

Forsyth tried a different tack. "All due respect, mister, I think you need to try for some of that sleep you can't seem to find. I doubt coffee's helping much." Over by the counter the two other men stood and stretched their backs. They settled caps on gray heads and made their way into the night. Forsyth caught furtive glances from both of them. A stream of cool air slipped inside. It had gotten colder as well as darker.

They sat in silence and watched the pair of old truckers pass in front of the building and dissolve into the encroaching shadows. Neither said as much but they were waiting for their rigs to chug into life, for the big headlights to cut the gravel dust.

Quiet rippled. Forsyth thought that maybe another light had fizzled out. The far end of the diner felt like another county.

The trucker looked at him. "I think those gaps between places are filling up. Something's looking for us. Couple of weeks back my mama started talking to me on the CB." He kept swiveling his coffee cup, only now Forsyth was almost glad for the sound. "I know what you're thinking, and it ain't ghosts. My mama's alive and well. Lives in Charlotte and volunteers at the hospital." His eyes dropped to the table again and he drained the mug. Set it down and went back to turning it.

"Your mama got a radio?" Forsyth would have liked some coffee himself but the waitress had yet to come back up front.

"Nah, she'd hardly know what to do with one. But I hear her. Different channels too. She tells me to pull over sometimes, get out of the cab and walk into a field and look up at the stars. Just lie down there in a bed of grass. She talks about greener pastures waiting. Get out and walk into the night, Sally— that's what she calls me, Sally. Always seems to be when it's darkest, right in the crease between midnight and that first streak of morning."

Forsyth put his head in his hands. His expected thought—something along the line of getting away from this man and back on the road—wouldn't come to him. Somehow he found himself fixated on all the blank space in the world. He felt he'd known it for some time, from the corners of his eyes. There was an awful lot of it between here and Valdosta, even on the interstate. He kept his CB off as a rule, but would he flip it on tonight when he settled into the driver's seat?

He glanced outside again and saw another light in the eave had gone dark. Their corner of the lot was the only beacon left. The light inside the diner might as well have been held in a box. It stopped inches beyond the windows.

"Some nights I see people running up a ditch to the road as I drive by," Sally said, "or standing in the trees. I'd call them pale. I'd call them pale enough to glow, except they're not. They're as dark as the dark, but I see them just fine. And then the radio starts crackling and my mama's talking me out of the truck."

"Come on now," Forsyth said, "you got to know that's not your mama. What you're talking about sounds like sirens luring sailors to their deaths or something. I mean, CB isn't what it used to be, but people still play with it."

"Whoever it is, she knows I ran away when I was eight because she and Dad put my dog down. She knows the name of the magazine she found under my mattress a few years later. Dad, now, he died ten years ago. Cancer. Never been his voice coming out of the CB."

"How come I haven't heard of this? I'm on the road about as much as you." Forsyth wanted to laugh, but instead his mind got snagged on the rest area whose lot he'd napped in early that morning. Anonymous brick squatting in the drone of highway traffic and Georgia pines scenting the air. All those unnoticed trees. Over the years he'd relieved himself in hundreds of those facilities. He'd bought undrinkable coffee, washed the sleep out of his eyes, even jerked off once or twice to clear his head. Lonely places, yes, Sally was right. He felt the deeper possibility of it unfurl in his head like a fever.

But no matter how empty a diner found itself, it wasn't a rest stop. It had a pulse. A constant heartbeat. He craned his neck to look for the absent waitress again.

"Well, now you have. I didn't know until Hitch told me." Sally's grin was both sly and shameful. His lips stayed pressed together inside the nest of beard. It was the first time his face had come alive with something other than a jittery fear.

"Those two guys haven't started up their rigs yet," Forsyth said. He'd meant to just change the subject, clear that leering smile from Sally's face, but realized he was speaking one notch above a whisper. Both of them watched the black humps of the trucks still as felled trees in all that shadow. "Probably napping. Or napping with each other."

Neither man cracked a smile.

"Tonight Mama said I should stop here and rest a while. Lay my troubles on a kindred spirit, is how she put it. I don't think they like the voices of the dead. On account of the dead are the ones we've let go of." Sally pushed his cup away and stood up. "This place does seem like one of those gaps. It's not like there's much of anything out here. But you wait until you leave. You'll get it now." He looked through the window again. "I gotta take a leak."

He shuffled toward the little hallway in back. Forsyth watched him push into the men's room. He got up himself and walked over to the coffee station, grabbed a mug and filled it. Found some half and half and a spoon. When he got back to the table he saw at once that the outside light above his booth's window was the only one still lit up. The dark gathered close, pressing against the glass, and he tried not to look for things shifting in it.

He poured the creamer in and stirred his coffee. The clink of the spoon unnerved him. It was too much like an alarm bell. He needed to be on the road now in order to have any chance of getting back to Little Rock by suppertime tomorrow. But he sat there, eyes dragging to the window then yanking away. He pictured the radio in his rig and could almost hear a sea of static, and what would he do if his own mother began calling out to him from her nursing home in Tucson, edging him toward the rocks?

The dark outside was too active and all four trucks sat buried under it. No reason they should have been silent. Those two grizzled truckers would idle their engines on a cold night. He'd never met one who wouldn't. Diesel ran long.

In the window he could see the restaurant's reflection, so he watched both the lot and the hallway behind him while he waited for Sally to return. He thought of the stack of books he'd bought for Lizzie's birthday. Rachel would give him a real smile for those. Their daughter was going to hit kindergarten running. And when he wheeled in the purple bicycle at the end, right around the time Lizzie thought the presents were done for the year… well, he figured Rachel might have something more than a smile to offer.

Forsyth sat there and Sally didn't come back. He kept his eye on that last bulb shining out in the dark. A white face might have drifted into sight before retreating. He wasn't sure. The key to his rig was heavy in his pocket.

In the other pocket his phone buzzed. He jumped in his seat before fishing it out. Nothing on the screen, not even "incoming call." He tapped the phone and held it up to his ear and listened.

"Daddy?" Lizzie's voice came as though she were sitting in his lap. "Daddy!"

"Baby?" His mouth went dry. "What are you doing up? You need to be in bed, hon." He said the normal things, the daddy things, his fingers pinching the bridge of his nose hard enough to hurt.

"I'm not sleepy. Come outside, Daddy. I'm in the trees."

"No, baby, you're not in the trees. You're dreaming." He started touching everything on the table, coffee cup, plate, silverware. He gripped the napkin dispenser in his hand and tried to squeeze it into something else. An anchor, anything to keep him fastened to his seat. He shouted Sally's name into the empty diner.

"He's with his mommy. Come outside, Daddy. It's my birthday. It's tomorrow now."

Forsyth nearly fell to the floor as he lurched out of the booth. He staggered across the room and down the short hall and banged into the restroom.

Empty, it could have always been empty but for the window half-open in the wall above the urinal. Cold air, somehow darkened air, fell through it. The tube lights in the ceiling fizzed. He slammed the window shut and checked the single stall. A strip of tissue was draped over the toilet.

"Told you, Daddy. Come look at the stars with me. They're birthday stars."

He clamped the phone to his ear as he went back to the counter, stood by the register a moment, then pushed through the swinging door into the kitchen. "Hello?" he called. The waitress had to be here. A cook, somebody. But there was only a low murmur of talk radio voices from the back. They faded into a wash of fuzz and then his older brother whispered his name. Paul, who lived way up in Vancouver. They'd talked on the phone just last week. Forsyth heard his name again, louder, and fled back into the dining area.

"You're not my Lizzie," he said into the phone.

"Please, Daddy." His daughter's one-more-story voice, the one he'd been longing to hear, perfect down to the pleading end. "Come finish. I want to know if the pigs go outside to the wolf."

A hinge creaked behind him from the kitchen door. Soft breaths from the phone, waiting. He pictured his little girl tucked under a furry blanket six hundred miles away, green eyes peeking out, the spill of her fine light hair. He pictured her needing him, heaved a deep breath and stepped out into the close cold of the night.

Just get to the truck and out of this creepy place. His keys were in one hand, the phone still raised in the other. A tiny gleam of light reflected off his chrome grille, a hint of red side panel, and he fixed his eyes on it. Just get to the truck. The shoulder of his jacket whispered along the wall of the diner and he jerked away from it.

A small, bright laugh came from somewhere close. He heard it in his ear in the same instant. Rustling ahead, the faint crunch of gravel. When he reached the corner, the vast black space opening before him, he paused and looked up. No moon hung in the endless stars. That one light in the eave of the diner's roof had been holding on, bravely throwing out its white heaven for Forsyth. Now it flickered and winked and was gone.

AARON POLSON

The men do not have normal names like John or Tran or Jose.

Instead, they have names like Izzy and Duff and Rat. They all have scars. Bunny, a wiry guy, average height and built like a runner, wears a light pink mark, three inches, from his left earlobe diagonally down his jaw line toward his chin. Hair won't grow in the mark's path, so he stays clean shaven. Bunny earned his scar when he killed a bigger man, a biker in black leather jacket, jeans, and riding chaps, outside Slow Ride Roadhouse in Gimple, Tennessee. The biker wasn't a man anymore.

He was Bunny's first kill.

This is their job, these men with scars and no real names. They kill and live without names.

Bunny has one other scar, a burn mark on the inside of his left bicep. This one dates to his childhood, fourth grade, when his father held a cigarette to the flesh until it sizzled. Bunny didn't flinch. He knew he deserved the punishment for leaving a shovel in the garden during a rainstorm.

Some scars are on the inside, buried memories and hurt. Bunny has those, too, but the men are not allowed to show those scars. They are not men anymore. They can't be. They are machines. They are scarred and broken and heart-sore and raw from killing, but outside, they are machines with cold steel gazes. They are weapons in a war few know they are fighting.

They come to small towns in battered RVs and old Airstream campers. They follow the war where it takes them. They drive trucks to pull their homes. They wear denim and flannel and old t-shirts bearing the names of too many places to remember. All of the clothes come from secondhand

Haves and Have Nots

stores, Goodwill, the Salvation Army…they wear the clothing of a thousand people.

They are called things, case numbers or code words or monikers born from blood and mass graves and the gruesome count of bodies in their wake. They have memories of slit throats and crying mothers, nighttime wailing and prayers and vain curses. They have false titles, psychos or ghouls or monsters, and one which holds truthfulness but not the truth: murderers.

They are ghosts. They are heroes. They are necessary.

Bunny's first, the biker, was a big man who knew to duck when crossing through doorways. He stooped as he left Slow Ride smelling of cigarettes and gasoline. The wind had peeled away layers of skin leaving raw cheeks and red capillary webs. Two tufts of grey split his dark beard at either side of his chin. Tiny wrinkles pointed toward the corner of his eyes, surely lines earned with smiles and laughter and other things men do, but the biker wasn't a man anymore.

Bunny and the others had watched him for hours and had slipped into the lot when he paid his bill. Bunny tackled him and used the knife. The biker fought back like any living thing when faced with oblivion. His fingernails caught Bunny's cheek. There was pain and blood and a warm rush in Bunny's gut, the kind of sensation which came along with knowledge that he may have misjudged the biker's strength or the strength of what lived in the biker's body.

But the blood wasn't the biggest mess—not Bunny's or even the biker's.

The biker had a family.

This is how things go. The kills often have family, and family must be cleaned, too. Under the half-moon in the gravel lot outside Slow Ride, Bunny held a rag to his bleeding face while Rat, Izzy, and Duff bagged the body to the back of a truck. Cupcake found the wallet. He found the pictures of a daughter and a wife with names written in black ink on the back.

"Hey," he said. "Hey…this guy has a kid."

Bunny pulled the rag away from his face and examined the blood.

"So we gotta…"

Bunny nodded.

And this is how firsts go. Bunny's was a large man once, but then he was something else. "Bunny's turn," they said, knowing each had their turn, their first. Firsts are hard. Firsts are difficult and bloody and messy and too easy to forget they aren't human anymore. Because firsts bleed like people. Firsts wear favorite t-shirts and tattoos like people. Firsts have scars, too, places where they cut their legs on barbed wire trying to jump pasture fences as children. Firsts have wallets with pictures of family members in them or old condoms stuffed between dollar bills and receipts from two years ago as if that pair of jeans will ever be returned.

Firsts were human. Firsts still smell like humans, and so do seconds, thirds, and so on.

But they smell like something else, too, something ancient and musty and dead but not dead.

"Your turn," Bunny told Cupcake. "Your Turn."

The men do not have families.

They do not have pictures in their wallets of children or wives or even girlfriends. They burn these things before joining the small caravan. If the photos existed, they were dust and memory, old pictures from before some bleak event, an accident, an illness, irrevocable differences…

Bunny's dad, the man who scarred Bunny's bicep with a cigarette, burned to death in his mobile home. The fire spread quickly, too quickly for an accident in the kitchen. Bunny was seventeen and standing outside as it burned. He didn't dial 911. His parents were divorced—had been since Bunny was eight—and the little house with the garden in which he'd left the shovel in the rain belonged to his mom and a string of failed relationships. She'd brought boyfriends, broken men who worked long physical hours in the sun and sucked life from beer cans or whiskey bottles, into the house in a steady stream since nine. The first had touched Bunny at night, touched him in a way which heaped shame on his nine-year-old shoulders and left a scar without a long pink line.

Before he joined the caravan, Cupcake carried a photo similar to the biker's. His showed three people: him as a younger man, a thin woman with limp, dishwater blonde hair, and a little boy. The Cupcake with a family had been named Tim and his hair was thick and brown and wavy, but the men do not have families. Cupcake's bled to death on I-80. The caravan found him on the angry end of grief, face down in a Motel 6 bathroom in Cedar

Rapids after months of pills and no prescriptions. He was broken enough to put back together like they needed him.

They called him Cupcake because his hair still waved in a long swoop like icing.

They do not have families because families take up space. They clog brains and slow actions. Clogged brains and slowed actions would mar their purpose. Clogged brains and slowed actions would turn scars into fatal wounds.

Bunny and Cupcake found the address in the biker's wallet and followed its trail to his house while the others burned his body. They always burn bodies, more tradition than necessity because death comes for everything the same way, no matter how ancient. The men understand, even in a faint, soft-edged way, the universe will eventually die. Oblivion waits for everything; they simply bring it sooner. This is how they feel connected. This is how they maintain armor against that which would rob their humanity in the midst of intimate but unthinkable work.

The biker's house was small, a little yellow ranch with half-brick façade in front. On Tuesday night, the wife and daughter would be home. Bunny knew it and Cupcake knew it because being one of the men in the caravan, no matter how new, gave you certain knowledge. The knowing existed before the joining, flashes of thought and future memories which grew fungus-like and haunted their brains.

Like how Bunny knew his father's trailer would burn. He hadn't set the fire, but woke with the image and ran three miles from his mother's place to feel the heat. Like how Cupcake knew his family was dead when he woke even though the semi-trailer wouldn't jackknife in front of his wife's Honda Accord for another four hours.

Could he have called to warn her?

No. Being one of them—carrying their burden—means knowing nothing will change oblivion. All they can do is make life better for the rest of us. They have our burdens in their bodies, in their brains, in their every action. The men have deep wells in which those burdens are lost.

They have instruments, too. They use knives because killing is intimate. Killing is messy and real and they do not want to forget why they do what they do.

"Ready?" Bunny asked Cupcake as he slowed their truck at the address from the biker's wallet.

"Ready."

"Your turn, but I get one of them," Bunny said, holding a quarter in one hand. "Heads or tails. Winner picks."

The men do not have many things, but they have scars. They have scars and stories and the stories hold them together. They fill in the spaces between what the men are now and what they once were. Stories explain cigarette burns and raw patches on knees. Stories tie them together, stories of empty seats at dinner and grey burial skies, stories of bleeding knuckles and beer-soaked curses. Stories of little red pills and the antiseptic smell of motel bathrooms.

They have heartbreak and brokenness but they know the need for all of it. They know being broken keeps others from being broken. They are the first wave on shore, the fodder for body bags and shallow graves. They are the reason we sleep at night, the reason we can raise glasses at holiday parties or weddings or birthdays and pretend the blackness outside our nighttime homes holds no monsters. They have shed all hope but this: the rest of us can forget oblivion and live in the light.

The men have purpose.

The biker's home smelled of cinnamon, only a thin layer that scarcely covered the ache of death underneath. Bunny nosed it and so did Cupcake. They exchanged a glance in the foyer of the house, both listening for anything, footsteps, tell-tale inhuman sounds, even human voices. The lock had given easily, but such things always made noise.

Bunny nodded toward the left and a small hallway.

Cupcake followed.

Seconds were easy, and Bunny knew it even before he slit the wife's throat. She lay in the bed, panting too quickly for even a plump woman in her late 30s. She was not human, and they both knew. They knew before leaving the parking lot of Slow Ride, before entering the bar after locating the biker.

Nothing wants to die, and the thing inside the woman fought. She beat her arms against Bunny's shoulders, trying to scream but only managing a wet, bubbling sound because of the thick gash and broken windpipe. Bunny pressed a knee into her chest. The thrashing slowed as he sawed through to bone. Cupcake held her legs in place, held until they went limp and drew his hands away. Pale marks appeared where his hands had been, but the blood drained quickly.

They keep us safe. They do work we cannot do. The work is not glamorous or beautifully choreographed like killing in Hollywood. Killing spills real blood. Real death gurgles and flails about, arms thrashing. Killing is personal, even though the one's they kill are no longer people. Killing is intimate, up close.

The men lie to each other about killing. The men are not machines, and they know it. Their dreams wear nightmare's inky cloak. They know killing until they are killed. They know they have to be machines so we can sleep peacefully in our homes, free of unimaginable things which would open our skulls to crawl inside.

But they are not machines, no matter how we might imagine.

They are men.

They had families. They had hope. They had everything we do but it's gone, all of it, so they know the loss and know that for which they fight.

Bunny and Cupcake drove away before the house started to burn. They'd spread enough gasoline next to the bodies to be sure both would go early in the blaze, early enough they'd be ash before first responders arrive in a swirl of sirens and shouts. This was how they left the remains of the biker's family. This is how they always planned to work: quick and efficient and with enough fire to leave all their efforts in ash.

But ashes tell lies.

Ashes cover moments of hesitation and the mess of blood. Ashes make men seem cold or calculating or efficient when the truth bears tears and bitter memories and a long list of names they will never forget.

They have no regrets but plenty of remorse. They know the truth and hate it.

They have memories.

Fifteen minutes before the blaze, before the well-placed gasoline and slow burning fuse made of oil-soaked rag, Cupcake stood next to what used to be a little girl, knife in hand, as Bunny waited at the foot of the bed. Stuffed animals filled the room—elephants, unicorns, monkeys, but only one on the bed, a blue walrus. The nightlight outlined the scene, filled the room with a warm, yellow glow for the audience of stuff animals to watch an execution. The walrus under the girl's arm stared at Cupcake.

But the room did not smell like a little girl's.

There was something in her, something cold and black and alien but more terrestrial than humans, more ancient than any of us, sleeping inside her skull. She was not a little girl. She was something as old as Earth buried in a little girl's skin.

Cupcake knew before they parked in front of the house. He'd known before they saw the photo in the biker's wallet. He'd known months ago when the others found him face down in the Motel 6 bathroom. He closed his eyes and thought of his wife and son and the last moment before they died.

He still loved her. He loved the boy, too. Sam. Samuel, after his grandfather.

Machines don't have memories.

He was not a machine. Neither was Bunny. Neither were any of the men—not Rat or Izzy or Duff out with the trailers and the ashes of the biker. They were men, and men raged against the night. Men flailed their arms against their own insignificance in a blind universe. Men raged against ancient things neither evil nor good, but like men only wanting a little more time before oblivion swallowed those things, too.

Only humans could do the work: murderers, of monsters.

These were Cupcake's thoughts as he stood at the girl's bedside with the knife.

APPEARANCES

CRAIG D.B. PATTON

"Time to go to sleep, sweetie." Kurt said, rising after bestowing the final bedtime kiss.

Natalie seized his hand. It often startled him how small and delicate she was. The bones just beneath the warmth of her skin felt bird-like. "Will you stay until I fall asleep?"

"Yes," he said. He knew that if he protested, if he tried to say anything more at all, his voice would betray him. He settled back down on the edge of her bed.

"Okay." She closed her eyes.

He could just see her face by the light spilling in from the lamp at the top of the stairs. Darkness did not hold the room completely. Not yet. Kurt sat in the gloom and waited. Waited and watched for the tiny night-blooming flower of her mouth to open. Waited and listened for her breathing to change. While he waited he surveyed the room, careful to move gently. The paper on her easel was a blank gray rectangle. Her doll house sat closed in the corner. Daniel, her teddy bear, was lying on the floor near her desk. She usually took him to bed. It was normally one of his roles to help her fall asleep. But now... He looked at Natalie. Well, now she wanted a hand that held hers back.

It did not take long before she fell asleep.

Kurt paused in the doorway and gazed at the small bundle of his child— his *only* child now. Putting her to bed felt like unfinished business. He worried each night that there was something left unsaid, something more he should have done. He hated leaving her there alone in the dark now. Because you just never knew. The world was cruel and took what it wanted with no warning.

He closed the door and turned to look at the open wound of Matthew's room. His son's green and white striped soccer jersey lay on the rug draped in shadows ten feet from the door. They had decided to leave it, to leave everything the way it had been that day. Just for now. Just until they knew what to do. Even the twisted remains of his bicycle lay on a table beneath a tarp.

He walked downstairs. The bouquets and condolence cards piled on the console table came into view. Most of the flowers had wilted—heads bowed, faces pinched like the people who had brought them.

As was their custom, Kurt opened a bottle of wine and went in search of Jodi. She was sitting at the dining room table, the backlog of bills spread in a crescent moon around her laptop.

He held up the bottle. "Would you like a glass?"

"God yes." She kept working.

He poured both glasses and sat down. He waited.

After a while Jodi finally glanced at him. "Sorry." She sat back with a sigh. "Forgiveness," Jodi said, holding her glass aloft.

His brow furrowed. "Of?"

"Me."

"I don't understand."

She set the glass down. "I've been awful these past couple of weeks. How many times have I snapped at you?"

"For God's sake, Jodi, we're going through hell. I think we should get a free pass on how we act."

"I'm not comfortable with that, Kurt. If it doesn't bother you, that's fine. But Natalie deserves better. What are we telling her if we can't keep it together?"

"I really do think you're handling this as well as anyone could."

She studied him a moment. "Okay."

The pool of silence stilled around them while they drank. He looked up at the ten balloons floating against the ceiling, each sporting a short tail of red ribbon. Matthew's birthday balloons. Kurt had filled and tied them to his son's chair while decorating the dining room. At the end of the day Matthew had cut them loose. Kurt's heart hurt remembering Matthew's delighted laugh as the balloons soared up and bounced around the ceiling.

He finished his glass, noticed that Jodi had already done the same and refilled both. "How's it going?"

She surveyed the piles. "I think we're mostly okay. Late on one credit card."

"Bet you if we call they'll waive the fees."

"I'm not calling some stranger to ask them to cut us a break because of what happened."

He wondered how many different ways they had said Matthew died without actually saying it. The phrase *because of what happened* was in frequent use. So was *our situation* and that old classic *our loss*. The wake had been a litany of such phrases along with *a terrible tragedy*. A slow, endless parade of people dressed in black, faces dripping grief as awkward platitudes tumbled from their mouths.

"Hey."

He blinked at her. "Hmm?"

"Where'd you go?"

"Sorry. I was thinking about the wake."

"Oh."

He emptied his glass and reached for the bottle.

Jodi held her glass aloft, as though unsure what to do with it. "The school psychologist wants to meet with us tomorrow at nine, remember."

"I know."

He leaned back and sipped his wine. Motion drew his gaze upward. One of the balloons was drifting slowly across the ceiling. The cherry red one. Matthew's most recent favorite color. His last favorite color. Kurt watched it sail above Jodi's head toward the door to the front hall.

"One's making a break for it."

Jodi looked where he nodded and watched it.

The balloon stopped where the ceiling met the wall, just to the left of the door frame.

Kurt tutted. "Well," he said to the balloon. "So much for your dreams of a bold future out in the world. Life's full of disappointments."

Jodi looked at him, her expression a bottomless chasm of loss. She snapped the laptop shut, rose, and walked out.

Kurt sighed. Stupid thing to say. He slumped back and looked at the balloons. "Forgiveness," he said, holding his glass up.

Cutting birthday balloons loose was a tradition in Kurt's side of the family. You could tell it was an important tradition, he explained, because they could not agree when it had started. Just a way to mark the end of the day, perhaps. But Kurt liked to think of it as something more.

"You know how you make a wish before you blow out the candles on the cake?" he had said to the children one year.

They had nodded and murmured agreement.

"Well, what do you wish for?"

They had protested at that. "Daddy, you're not supposed to tell!"

"Right. Sorry. What I mean is, do you wish for the world to be a better place? Do you wish for things for other people?"

Matthew had begun to look a bit worried at that, anticipating a rebuke. Jodi had taken his hand and smiled reassurance, knowing full well where this was going.

"No," Kurt had gone on. "We wish for things for ourselves. I do it too. And that's okay. It's our birthday, after all. But when our day is over, we go on with our lives. So, when we release the balloons, it's like we're offering ourselves to the world. We say, here I am, all five or eight or thirty-nine or..."

Jodi had arched an eyebrow.

"...however many years of me. Thank you. I'm going to go out into this new year and be the best person I can and the world will be better for it."

It was all a bit metaphysical for the kids, of course. They just wanted cake and to watch the balloons fly. But he valued the simple ritual of it. Perhaps Jodi did as well and had not simply been humoring him over the years

In the morning, Natalie woke him at the usual 7:01am. For an instant the past two weeks remained shrouded in the fog of sleep. But Natalie had news. "Daddy, Matthew's balloons are in the hallway downstairs. Come see."

Kurt eased out of bed and slumped downstairs. On the ceiling were four of the balloons: two blues, a yellow, and the cherry red.

"How did they get there?" Natalie asked.

He rubbed his eyes to drive the blur of sleep from them. "They floated there."

"How?"

"Hmm?"

"How did they move?"

It was earlier than he liked to take up his mantle as parental font of all knowledge and wisdom. He typically demanded a shower and a cup of coffee first. It was in the contract somewhere. But there was his daughter, gazing up at him. "Well. I think it's the air currents. The air conditioning comes on and sends little gusts of wind around."

She scowled. "How come mine never move?"

"We don't usually leave them this long. Yours would do the same thing if we left them."

"Why are we leaving them?" But she knew an instant later. "Because Matthew died?"

He nodded. "We just want to leave them for now."

She considered that for a moment. "Will they move more?"

"I don't know. Probably, I guess."

"Okay." And as if it were the most normal thing in the world and not freighted with an ounce of grief she headed for the kitchen to make her lunch for school.

Maybe she would be alright. Or maybe she at least had more of a chance to be all right than they did. He would accept that deal if it were offered. If at least one of his children survived to become a healthy adult that would be victory enough for him.

The next challenge to healthy survival came when he took Natalie to the bus stop in the morning. A nudge, an inaudible word, and all of the adult conversation stopped and the knot of mothers turned to watch them approach. The other children, sensing the change, stopped chattering and racing. They called their greetings to Natalie and she answered them softly back. He looked down at her, squeezed her hand, and smiled as convincingly as he could when she looked up. Natalie's smile wobbled but he let go of her hand anyway and she went and joined the other children.

The mother geese clucked their greetings.

"Hello."

"Welcome back."

"How are you?"

Their eyes were wide and doleful, brimming with their need to convey the depth of their sympathy.

The dishonesty of these exchanges annoyed Kurt. What they really meant was how very, very grateful they were that they did not live in the valley of shadows that he and Jodi did. It wasn't sympathy. It was closer to fear. The arbitrariness of Matthew being killed by a texting driver terrified them. It was an unwelcome reminder of just how vulnerable they and their children still were in this comfortable town.

He answered their social niceties in kind and wondered who was more grateful when the conversation shifted back to the perpetual onslaught of PTA and fundraising events.

That night he made pizza with just pepperoni and red pepper, Natalie's favorite. He added a side salad so Jodi would not complain the meal lacked color. He needn't have bothered. She hardly seemed to notice the food at all.

"Things go okay at work?" he ventured.

"Fine."

"Hmm. Not sure I'm buying that."

She shot him a look. He decided to revisit the topic later.

Jodi turned to Natalie. "How was your day, Natalie?"

"Fine."

Kurt could not quite suppress a smile.

If she saw it, Jodi ignored him. "Did Ms. Munson give you the assignments you missed?"

Natalie scowled at her. "Yes. It's going to take me years to catch up."

"Probably more like days," Jodi said.

"Years are made out of days," Natalie grumbled, flopping back and staring at the ceiling.

Kurt actually started to laugh for the first time since Matthew's death. He couldn't help it. Didn't want to help it. It felt glorious.

"Matthew's balloons are gone," Natalie said.

It was like the air froze. All the joy he felt frosted instantly to the walls. They looked up. The ceiling was empty.

"Did you take them down?" Jodi demanded.

Kurt held up his hands. "No. Easy. They just started drifting around that's all." He explained. Natalie chimed in, having remembered their conversation that morning.

Jodi's agitation waned into puzzlement. "So...they're still here."

He nodded. "Should all be in the house unless one snuck out when we opened a door."

Natalie bounded out of her chair. "Let's go find them!"

They joined her impromptu game. Two balloons were in the foyer. Three were around the corner in the hall beside the stairs and a white one had found its way up the stairs themselves. Two others hovered in the living room and a yellow one was in the downstairs bath above the sink. But the red one was still unaccounted for when Natalie went to take her bath.

"Read to me," she said to Kurt. It was the first time she had asked him *since that awful day.*

"What would you like?"

"We were reading..." Her face twisted into her most determined expression, mouth clamped shut, cheeks slightly puffed, as though holding her breath to plunge deep into her memories. "You know. The one with Peter and Lucy and Edmund and...the other girl—"

"Susan. *The Lion, the Witch, and the Wardrobe.*"

"That's it! And the girls had snuck after Aslan when he went to meet the White Witch."

"Let's read something else tonight." Something cheerier, he thought, like Edward Gorrey or something from *A Series of Unfortunate Events*.

She protested until he suggested *A Bear Called Paddington*. Good old Paddington. It didn't matter that Natalie knew the book word for word.

Kurt took up his accustomed perch on the chair just outside the bathroom door which Natalie left ajar to provide enough privacy while still being able to hear. Mr. and Mrs. Brown had just named the lost bear after the London railway platform where they had found him when Kurt glanced up. The missing red balloon hovered in the open doorway to Matthew's room. It hung there in the air just a dozen feet from him.

"Dad?" Natalie called.

"Sorry," he called back and resumed reading. But after a few sentences he looked up again. The balloon had come out into the hall. It drifted toward him along the landing. Kurt closed the book and listened. He heard Natalie's splashing from the tub. He heard the clinking of silverware and the clatter of plates downstairs as Jodi put dishes in the dishwasher. And then beneath it all he picked out the soft, steady whoosh of the central air system. The balloon was riding the air currents. Just like he had said. As if to provide further proof, the white balloon at the top of the stairs began to shuffle along the ceiling.

"Dad!"

"Sorry."

"What are you doing?"

"Watching the balloons."

The water sounds stopped. "What?"

"I said I'm watching the balloons."

"Are they moving?"

"Yes."

"I want to see." A sloshy tsunami of sounds began.

"No. You need to take your bath. You—"

Natalie's head appeared around the edge of the door. Her face glistened with water and her matted hair was covered in suds. "Where?"

He rolled his eyes, sat back and waved at them.

"Oh." She drew out the word, tracing it over a broad hill and down. Her eyes grew very wide. Kurt knew that look well. It was the expansive sense of wonder she viewed the world through.

"Hello," she said, smiling at the balloons.

Kurt worried sometimes that Natalie had an overdeveloped taste for fantasy. It had been part of the conversation with the counselor just that morning.

"Of course, we should anticipate that she may withdraw socially for a while," Ms. Benson had said. "Or that her behavior may become erratic at times. Anything could happen, really."

The statement had reeked of pseudoscience. "What do you mean?" Kurt had asked.

Ms. Benson had smiled gently. "We've talked before about her difficulties forming friendships with peers. She has an active, wonderful imagination that she uses in every situation. Sometimes her flights of fancy last longer or are stranger than most children her age want. Now she has to process the loss of her brother—"

Process...as if Matthew's death was iron ore, just a load of raw material to refine into something more useful.

"—and it's quite natural for her to use her imagination to do so. In the absence of significant friendships she will need to do her healing on her own. With all of our support of course. We should be careful not to put too many boundaries around her behavior for now."

All of which meant that if Natalie wanted to stop taking a bath to watch balloons float in the hallway, Kurt should let her. He watched the red one arc over the stairwell and gracefully descend out of view.

After they had tucked Natalie into bed, Kurt and Jodi retired to the living room. Jodi stared into the shifting high definition expanse of the television. Kurt pretended to read. Two balloons slipped in from the hallway and joined them. One went to the mantle and stopped against the large print of Monet's *Water Lilies* that hung above it. The other rose to the ceiling and drifted past them out of view.

Kurt redoubled his effort staring at the words in front of him. If he could do that long enough he thought he might make it through one sentence and then another and perhaps even enough of them to necessitate turning a page.

It would be nice to turn a page.

"I got three emails today encouraging me to sign Matthew up for activities," Jodi said.

He gaped at her. "What? From who?"

She continued staring into the unblinking eye of the television. "Parks and Rec for basketball, the library for a new sixth grade reading group, and the aquarium's having early registration for winter vacation camps. He loved that sting ray camp last year."

"I'm sorry."

"I guess I should tell them to take us off the mailing list, but..."

A tiny tremor rattled Jodi's jaw. Kurt set the book down and put his arm around her shoulders. They were smaller now, sharper. He could feel the sob rattling deep inside her. "Someday."

"It was awful at work," she blurted.

"What happened?"

Jodi shrugged. "It feels silly. Everyone was just trying to be nice, you know? Asking me how I was doing, saying how sorry they were..." She looked at him. "But it just felt so empty. How do they *think* I'm doing, you know?"

He nodded. "I know exactly what you mean."

She shook her head to shut him up. "But it's more than that. I swear I sat staring at my computer half the day without doing anything. I talked to people on the phone and then couldn't remember what we'd said after I hung up. All day I just felt so...numb."

Kurt waited to be sure that she was done and that it was his turn to talk. He told her about the bus stop that morning and shared his own account of awkward coworker sympathies. "I suppose it's normal," he said. "People think they have to say something, even if they don't really understand. It'll pass."

The balloon that had drifted across the ceiling reappeared in the periphery of his vision. It sank and hovered a few inches above one of the potted plants on the console table behind them. He had a sudden urge to tap it away from them.

Jodi turned and looked at it. She almost smiled. "Matthew would have liked the way they're moving around the house. How long do you think they'll do that?"

She was right. Matthew would have enjoyed the whimsy of the balloons' behavior. "I don't know. A few days? They're getting smaller. Losing gas. That's why they don't stay on the ceiling anymore."

They watched it move off again, settled back into isolated silence, and eventually went to bed. Kurt never did turn a page.

The next day felt even more contrived to him than the one before. A piece of bad theater cast with failed actors who knew it was a lousy script and let it show. Having already expressed their condolences and offered their support the day before, his coworkers withdrew to banal routines. He watched the clock a lot and left ten minutes early.

Natalie was crying when she came off the bus that afternoon.

"What's the matter?" he asked, dropping to one knee to enfold her.

"Not sure what's up," the driver called out the door. "She was crying when she got on at the school."

Kurt nodded. "Thanks."

The bus pulled away and the other families scattered like startled birds, leaving them alone on the corner. "Shhhhh," he soothed, stroking her hair. "Easy, baby girl. I gotcha. Do you want to tell me what happened?"

She shook her head, buried her face deeper in his chest. Kurt waited a bit before he stood and led her home by the hand. The dam burst as they reached the front step.

"Trevor Andrews was...was, tuh...tuh...teasing me."

A boy in her class. No one she'd had trouble with before, as far as he knew. "About what, sweetie?"

"He suh...said I was stupid for talking to Matthew."

He stiffened. "When was this?"

She started to regain her equilibrium. "On the playground. I was under the playscape and I guess he heard me and then on the way to the bus he said I was weird because I talk to dead people. And everyone was *looking* at me, Dad."

For the sake of Trevor Andrews and his entire family, Kurt was very glad he was the one hearing the story first and not Jodi. Hell hath no fury like a woman scorned, he sometimes said, except for a woman defending her child. Kurt was angry, but he wasn't about to drive to the offending child's home and confront the family, something Jodi had done once after a preschool bully beat up Matthew. Mostly, Kurt wanted to comfort Natalie. He settled her at the dining room table with a slice of raspberry pie and a glass of milk and only then did he call the school and speak with the principal. She made all the appropriate sympathetic statements and assured him that she would follow up the next day with both Trevor and his family.

When he hung up Natalie was standing behind him in the doorway to the dining room. "Can I go play?"

He appraised her. No sign of distressed child remained. "Do you have any homework?"

"Just some reading."

"Okay, well, make sure you leave time for that."

"Okay." She turned and scampered off.

He set about making dinner, grateful once again for the capacity of his daughter to repel the barbs that life forced into her skin.

Kurt had just put the lasagna in the oven when the doorbell rang. UPS delivered an LL Bean package of fall clothes his parents had sent for Natalie. When he closed the door he heard her talking upstairs. He paused and listened, wondering whether she was talking to Matthew and what she was saying to him if she was. Natalie sounded happy but her voice was low. He couldn't make out the words.

He started softly up the stairs, easing his foot onto each step. A twinge of guilt pricked him. Matthew had caught him doing this once. Kurt had suspected him of being on the phone with a girl, talking about who knew what, which meant it could possibly maybe be things that he and Jodi were not remotely ready for their son to be talking about, especially to girls. Kurt had made it halfway up before Matthew snatched the door open and popped out like an enraged figurine in a cuckoo clock.

"You were listening to me!"

"Maybe a little."

"That's invasion of privacy!"

"Son, I'm going to be invading your privacy until you go to college. Possibly until you're thirty."

Standing there now listening to Natalie he ached with loss. He would give anything for the chance to make good on the threat.

Natalie's door was open. She did not pop out but he could hear her clearly now.

"Would you like honey or sugar?" she asked.

A tea party. He smiled. Natalie held extravagant tea parties with her stuffed animals. He had not been invited to one in at least a year. The first bit of shyness about them perhaps, a sense that they were the play of a younger child. Or maybe he had offended his host. Slurped or spilled his imaginary tea. He reached her door at the top of the stairs and looked in.

Natalie sat in the middle of the floor amid a ring of balloons. Five of them hovered there at different heights. The white and yellow ones on either side of her had faces and thatches of hair scrawled on them in marker. All of them, he noticed a moment later, had faces and hair.

"Hi, Daddy," Natalie said.

Something fluttered in his mind on dark and dusty wings. He looked at her, considering his words. "Hi sweetie. You having fun?"

"Uh huh. Do you want to join us?"

He did not. He wanted to be downstairs. He wanted to be making a salad while listening to NPR. "I have to make dinner. Were all these balloons in here?" The question leapt out of him.

"Uh huh. I think they wanted to play."

He nodded and excused himself to check the oven, ashamed at his discomfort. It was ridiculous. She was just playing. If Matthew was alive he would be playing with her right now. He had been so good with her. When Natalie's teacher had asked the class to make a "Heart Chart" by drawing a large heart and then filling it with the things that mattered most to them, Natalie had written "Family" at the top of one bulge and "Matthew" at the top of the other. He was her best friend, she explained, so she could include him twice. When Natalie came home sad, Matthew stopped whatever he was doing. He listened to her and seemed to understand her better than Jodi or Kurt.

So what would Matthew have done? He would play along. Ask the names of the balloons. Sit down among them. Strike up conversation about life as a balloon. Joke about the types of food that filled him with gas. Kurt couldn't bring himself to do any of those things.

The missing limb of their family throbbed. Matthew was gone. They needed to fill the roles for each other that he once had. That meant learning how to do and be new things, even if it felt awkward and strange. Change was never easy. But it was essential to survival.

At dinner Kurt encouraged Natalie to tell Jodi what had happened at school. He thought Jodi handled the news well.

"Of all the insensitive things to say! The boy should be expelled."

"What does 'expelled' mean?" Natalie asked.

"It means you were so bad you're not allowed to be in school," Jodi said.

Natalie considered that. "So you stay home?"

"Usually. Yes."

"Like vacation?" Her eyes brightened. "Can I be expelled?"

Kurt smiled. "You're such a good influence," he said to Jodi with a wink before turning to Natalie. "It isn't any fun. Everyone else is in school so there's no one to play with and when you go back you have to catch up on all the work you missed."

She shrugged. A lost, helpless gesture. "I don't have anyone to play with anyway."

The words were a sucker punch to the gut. Kurt reeled. He couldn't breathe. He couldn't breathe and something needed to be said. Right now. But he could only flail in the despairing silence of the room.

"Oh, sweetie. You're going to make lots of friends," Jodi said, reaching across the table and taking her hand. "Sometimes it just takes a while to meet them."

Natalie looked at her. "Matthew said it's because I'm different and lots of people don't like different, so you have to wait for the people who do."

Kurt started crying. Great streams of tears. Just like that.

Jodi looked at him, her eyes wet as well. She gave him a tremulous smile and turned back to Natalie. "Your brother was very smart. And he loved you so, so much. Remember what he said."

"I will." And then she started crying as well.

As they sat there in tears, Kurt was startled to feel the thick clouds of their collective grief part for an instant. A ray of something bright forced its way through. Maybe even hope. And later, as he stood at the kitchen sink doing dishes, he thought perhaps they had indeed taken a tiny step together. The first of many needed to leave the darkness of these past two weeks behind.

Kurt looked out at the blackening orange of dusk. A single leaf danced and spun its way down. It was the first tumbling leaf of fall he had seen, although dozens dotted the yard. The leaf caught in the mesh web of the backstop Matthew had used to practice pitching. It caught there like a fly in a web.

Shadows lengthened. Nights grew colder. Plants withered and leaves fell. Each passing day brought the cold death of winter closer. It was inevitable. But it did not have to be the end. Beyond the frigid dark were light and warmth and new possibilities. One just needed to endure long enough to reach them.

Kurt was restless that night, tumbling down jagged slopes on the shadowy border of nightmare. He had eaten too much of the lasagna or perhaps drank too much wine and the result was a stew of indigestion. A little after one in the morning he woke and felt the contents of his stomach bubble and spit, sliding down the walls. He tried rolling onto his side, but he could never fall asleep on his side, only on his stomach. No, he had to get up and drink some water. Dilute the stuff into submission.

When he opened his eyes there was a balloon above him.

He stifled a cry. Jodi mumbled in her sleep and rolled over. The balloon floated above his knees. In the dim light the balloon was a sickly, dull shade of yellow. Its marker eyes were lopsided, mismatched ovals with no pupils. The nose was a dainty triangle, like something seen on a cartoon character. But the mouth was broad and open in a wide grin of eerily perfect slabs of teeth.

Kurt stared at it, his heart banging away in his chest. The balloon remained still. He slid out of bed and went to the bathroom.

He half expected to find another balloon lurking there, but he had the room to himself. Kurt drank several cups of water as the pounding of his heart eased back to a more normal beat. He sighed. Between the indigestion and the start the balloon had given him, he was wide awake now. He wouldn't be able to get back to sleep, he knew. Not for hours. Maybe not at all.

A shape moved in the shadows. He peered out along the landing and saw a balloon traversing the space between Matthew and Natalie's rooms. Kurt set the cup down and watched as the balloon disappeared into Natalie's room.

The door was not normally open. In fact, he was certain it had not been when he came upstairs for bed. Perhaps Natalie was having trouble sleeping tonight as well. Best to check on her.

Kurt felt his heartbeat quicken again as he walked along. The door was only a foot open. Just enough to accommodate his daughter. Or a balloon. He paused a moment, listening to the total silence before he nudged the door further open and stepped inside. The room felt warm and there was a faint unpleasant odor. It took him a moment to place it. He had last smelled it on Matthew's birthday. The pungent scent of rubber balloons.

As his eyes adjusted to the near total blackness of Natalie's room he saw them. There were rounded shapes all over her bed and many more in the air. Dozens of them. A short tail of ribbon dangled from each. Through them, he could just make out the shape of his daughter's head. She lay on her back, her hair splayed across the pillow. Beside her on the pillow rested a balloon. Even in the dark he knew that it was red and that, if he could see the face on it more clearly, he would recognize it.

So, when we release the balloons, it's like we're offering ourselves to the world.

Natalie's head turned. One of her small hands slid out, felt along until it found the ribbon of the balloon beside her and clutched it. It was all right, something whispered in him. His daughter was at peace.

ROCKPORT BOYS

MEGAN ARKENBERG

It's hard to stay haunted in California, she says, taking a slow drag on her cigarette. That hungry something is in her eyes again, the animal glint you saw in her smile under the gas station's fluorescents, only out here in the fading sunlight it looks a little softer. A little more like longing. You nod, shaking the last of the six-dollar Syrah into your glass, and lick the rim of the bottle. It tastes like aluminum foil. And she closes her eyes.

She's moved again, she says, put the mountains between her and the Pacific. The sunlight here feels hot, unfiltered and clean, almost chemical. Now the bad nights, when they come, ride in on rain and too much coffee. It was time to shift anyway, she figures—you can understand that. Four days a week, she loads the second-hand pickup truck with tomato plants, spring garlic or crates of persimmons and heads to the markets, down the straight country roads with numbers for names, the radio blaring in static-broken Spanish and sea glass rosary beads jangling from the rearview mirror. The rosary and the radio station came with the truck. You don't hear about Rockport, Gloucester or Dogtown out here, and nobody would recognize the names if you asked. Mostly, she keeps quiet.

She feels your eyes on her and shifts in her camp chair, which creaks with the movement. Where to start. She says this flat, not a question, not really wondering. When she opens her lips the smoke escapes in a rush, and the wind carries it south. San Francisco—the final c cracks in her throat—San Francisco, that's where she met him, though even then she'd known that whatever brought him there hadn't brought him to stay.

What brought her there, you want to ask, hearing the ghost of Arkansas or Tennessee sweetness in her voice. But you know, intuitively, that it's not part of this story.

She brought a photograph out of the trailer when she went in for matches for the citronella candles. It sits on the gravel between you now, the candle light guttering over five identical smiles. Purposely or not, the boys in the picture had arranged themselves symmetrically, tallest in the middle, heads slightly turned to display sharp cheekbones and jawlines. It was on his desk, she says, the day she met him. That's him, second from the right. But he doesn't look much different from the other four, the same soft, dark, side-parted hair over a high pale forehead, the same well-groomed eyebrows and round hazel eyes. Eyelashes so black and long your thoughts could get tangled in them, lips the color of watermelon candy.

Rockport boys, she says, they're New England all the way through. The air around them smells like burning leaves, old barn boards, the Atlantic Ocean. Their family trees are full of beautiful men who were hanged as witches or lost at sea, and all their houses are haunted. In her head, she calls them the Rockport boys, although the five of them came from all over Cape Ann, one from as far west as Ipswich. Hers, the second from the right, he was from Gloucester, the west side of the Annisquam river. Such New England names.

She doesn't have a name for those who love the Rockport boys, she adds. Except, perhaps, doomed.

The day she met him, in San Francisco, the fog rolling in thick with winter morning, she was carrying a shipment of pale, fluted orchids to a bookstore-come-coffee-house just off Valencia. Its name was an obscure and forgettable literary reference, its furniture a carefully curated collection of antiques. The flowers, bundled in clear cellophane and stuffed upright in a narrow cardboard box, looked breakable, like a delicate piece of ceramic. The bookstore's office was on the building's second floor, at the end of a narrow staircase that opened off the alley, and that morning, at the top of the stairs, the door on the right had been left ajar.

It was the wrong door. Some species of nonprofit organization, which helped pay medical bills for single parents, unmarried partners left off each other's insurance. There were four desks in the long white room, mismatched, as though they'd been rummaged from separate estate sales. He sat at the second desk from the back. The east-facing window let in a band of pink that sliced across the shoulders of his gray dress shirt. His hair lifted off his forehead as though he'd just run his fingers through it, the fine strands hyper-visible in the sunlight, like dust motes. He was ripping pages from a stack of carbon-paper triplicate forms, tossing the yellow sheets in a wire basket on the desk near his elbow, the remaining white and pink pages into an overflowing bin at his feet.

"Fuck," he said. He looked up, saw her staring.

"Excuse me?"

"No, sorry, not you. Just this—" He lifted a form from the top of the stack. "Rejected applications. This was a car accident on the Bridge. Little girl was sitting in the front seat, almost went through the windshield. It took twenty seven stitches to fix her eyebrow. But there's no money for that." He peeled the yellow sheet decisively from its siblings, set it in the basket, let the other two float down. They missed the bin, landed on the bare floorboards.

She'd figured out she was in the wrong room, and he must have too, seeing the embroidered flower company logo on the breast of her polo. But she stayed in the doorway, caught off-guard by his voice, which was so at odds with the precision of his shirt, his haircut, the neat marshalling of the pens in the mason jar beside his computer monitor, layered tallest to shortest.

"First week on the job?" she asked.

"No. Takes a bit longer than that to wear on you. It'll be my fourth month at the end of December." He leaned forward in his chair now, over the stack of unprocessed papers. She watched the light pick out the thin creases at the corners of his eyes. "What about you? How long have you delivered flowers?"

She felt herself smiling with an eerie sense of dislocation, as though she were looking down from a great distance. As an attempt to engage her in conversation, to get her to linger in the long, improperly insulated office that smelled faintly of drywall and liquid paper, it was transparent. And there she was, lingering. Doomed.

She came back to the office when their shifts ended, and they went downstairs to the coffee house, to the pair of blood-brown leather armchairs beneath the window in the back. A barista was setting orchids in miscellaneous glass vases on the café tables, the flowers interspersed with cut twigs and sheaves of dried wheat. The shape in her latte foam looked like a wishbone, or a dove. At the cash register there was a cardboard box of prints by some local artist, black ink on off-white paper, titles written in pencil on the back. The boy, whose name, he said, was Ethan, bought her one titled *Homeward #3*. It was a picture of the Bridge. She watched his eyebrows arch with his smile, thought of twenty-seven stitches, said nothing.

The first dream, if you can call it a dream, came that night. There was a woman's voice, not making words exactly, just *there*, thrumming beneath images of her delivery van, its floor littered with cardboard to-go cups and dying, shriveled petals; of her cluttered apartment kitchen, which the dream stretched out and filled with strangers; of Ethan, leaning towards her and laughing, his hair lifting off his forehead, one hand flat on the arm of her leather chair.

She woke near four in the morning and found her inner thighs covered in slick, watery blood. She stripped the bed mechanically and padded into the bathroom, cleaned herself up and stood at the sink, rinsing the sheets in cold water. The blood was thin and pale, with a faintly sour odor that made her stomach turn. Dim thoughts of anemia fluttered in the back of her head. She braced herself, almost listening for the arrival of cramps, but they didn't come. She put a clean sheet on the mattress, not bothering with a blanket, and drifted back into dreams.

She asked him about the boys in the picture. She'd seen it on his desk that first day and hadn't mentioned it, although it sparked her curiosity, those five coldly handsome faces, nearly identical above the knots of their candy-striped ties. Were they brothers? Of a sort, he said. Family of a sort. But it wasn't a pretty story.

They'd meant to walk up Valencia, that evening, but they found a bench in front of a deli on 24th that was closed for renovations and sat, talking, their thighs touching now and then as he shifted his slight weight, his shoulders rounding as he stretched his palms across his knees. She told him about her family. About the way she remembered her mother, always curled up on the couch as she tiptoed in after school, bruised brown eyes, exhausted from the night shift at a gas station convenience store. About the sister she hadn't seen in almost a decade, who had gone north, to Chicago or maybe Milwaukee, and started work in factory that made packing materials. About the uncle who had found a dead woman hitchhiker in a ditch beside a liquor store parking lot, ten years before she was born. They never found out who the dead woman was, and half the town became convinced it was the uncle that killed her.

"Not sure why I'm telling you this," she said. He was smiling at her, but the silver had gone out of his eyes. That's what it was like, she decided, like the eyes of a taxidermy animal, the mirrors behind them, or the silver backing they put on fake diamonds to make them come alive. Only sometimes with him the mirrors slipped, the silver peeled off, and his eyes were just glass.

"Ugly stories get out," he said. His voice sounded strangely childish, the words coming from the front of his mouth, as though he were afraid he might accidentally swallow them.

The blood kept coming, she adds. A clump of ash falls from the end of her cigarette, lands on her blue-jeaned thigh, and she flicks it away with a fingernail. Never stopped the whole time she knew him, or for a few weeks after; pale, watery, not really like menses. It got heavier for a while, and no amount of cold water or hydrogen peroxide could get it out of her underwear. She doesn't remember ever wishing the bleeding would stop, just wanting it out of her body. Out, out, out—she punctuates this with her fingernail dragging across denim, hip to knee.

"You're from one of those old families," she guessed, "the ones who can count the ancestors who came over on the Mayflower." He had just told her he'd grown up in Massachusetts.

"No," he said, drawing it out and laughing, his fingertips caressing the short brown neck of a bottle of Negra Modelo. "Jesus, Puritans?"

"Then witches. Salem witch trials."

He smiled at that.

They were up on the fire escape behind her apartment, a thin balcony of steel mesh painted lime green. He sat on an old yoga pillow, the flannel blanket from her couch draped around his shoulders. She leaned against the railing and let the cool, wet wind rake its fingers through her hair.

"I'm right, aren't I? You've got somebody in your family tree hung at Salem?"

"Sure," he said.

"Who?"

He shook his head, took a swig from the bottle.

"Come on, who? I bet I know her from the history books."

"It wasn't at Salem," he said. "And it wasn't a 'her.' And it wasn't witchcraft, exactly."

"Exactly?"

He still held the bottle to his lips. He closed his eyes, tipped his head back and drank, the amber beer spilling over his chin, dripping onto his sharp fog-colored collar. She thought maybe he wasn't going to answer. Then he set the bottle down on the mesh with a resounding clang.

"You ever hear of Cape Ann?"

She shook her head.

"It's up at the top of Massachusetts bay. Popular with tourists now, big on clams and whale-watching in the summer. In the center of the cape, there's this place, Dogtown. Old colonial settlement, abandoned soon after the Revolution. It's had its share of nastiness since then, murders, sexual assaults." He wiped at his chin with the back of his hand. "Even before then, I guess. In the late 1680s, this man, my great-grandfather times eight or whatever, he came to Cape Ann with his family. Settled in Gloucester as a rope-maker. Never said where he'd come from. One morning, they found him hanging from a black cherry tree in Dogtown. Wasn't even a Dogtown at the time—wasn't anything but a cluster of trees, and some rocks."

"He hung himself?"

He shrugged.

Somewhere ahead of her, overly stately waves of Victorian rooftops, the Twin Peaks curved up into cloud. Streetlights, warm and yellow, flickered on in rows like orderly stars.

"One suicide in three hundred years," she said, "isn't an especially ugly family history."

"There have been more," he said. Just that.

She opened this book once, she says, a brand new paperback right out of the bookstore, the spine still flat and uncreased. And on page 112, there was a streak of something thin and brown, almost in the margin. Like coffee. Maybe like blood. Unexpected and bizarre and anything but innocuous. That's what she was like, the crying woman, the woman who came with the dreams. A streak of horrible brown right where you didn't expect it.

She sat up in bed one night, not long after that evening on the fire escape. She had been dreaming about Ethan, dreaming about fucking him, and there she was, standing by the plywood bookshelf in the corner of the bedroom: a sad woman in brown. Her hands moved across the shelves, the spines of books, the votive candle in a blue glass cup, leaving a black, wet trail in the dust. She was crying, and the lap of her skirts was wet with something dark. There was a sound when she walked, a faint scuffing noise like something was dragging at her ankles.

The mattress creaked. She looked over at the bed, her eyes flat disks of silver in the street light. A moment later, she was gone.

"Your other four," she asked abruptly, watching the barista compact the ground espresso beans for their cappuccinos, "do they have the same story?"

He was flipping through the cardboard box of prints, the ones with titles penciled on the back, his fingertips skimming along the upper left corners. "Yes," he said, and paused, one picture pinned upright beneath his index finger. It took her a moment to recognize a record shop in Chinatown. "It's a pretty elite club, isn't it?"

"Suicidal depression running in the family?"

The barista raised her blonde eyebrows.

"Or a family curse," he said. The words came from the front of his mouth again, and he bared his teeth, and she couldn't tell if he was being serious.

They took their coffees to the back, the worn leather chairs. High on the window, behind the lace curtains, a brown spider was spinning her web across the cold, damp glass.

"So why are your families cursed?"

"Jesus. You won't lay off it, will you?"

"I'm a morbid fuck," she said. "And I think I believe you."

He rested his head on the back of his chair. Looked up at the flaking plaster of the ceiling, the antique curtains, the tiny industrious spider. "I thought—" He swallowed, started again. "I thought I had an idea, once. Or at least a hint. The five of us got talking one night. There was beer and pot and someone was blaring metal out of his shitty car speakers. And we figured out there was a nightmare, or not quite a dream, just this…this *experience* that all of us kept having."

She set her cup down on the end table.

"It's a crying woman," he was saying, "in an old-fashioned brown dress. She's bleeding, I think."

"And she makes a strange sound when she walks."

His head snapped forward. Two spots of dark purple-pink colored his cheeks, and as she watched, she could swear she saw the color drain. He let his head fall back against the leather.

"Fuck," he said. "*Fuck* you. Don't do that."

She drew her legs up onto the cushion. He flinched when her knee brushed his. "Guess I don't need to tell you that I had the same—experience."

He didn't respond.

"So what's it mean?"

"Would I be here if I knew?"

I don't know, she thought. Where's *here*?

They sat in tense silence, sipping cooling cappuccino. His candy-colored lips barely seemed to touch the cup. He was beautiful, she thought, like something fragile. Like a delicate piece of ceramic. And she longed, not to love him, but to protect him. Wanted that so badly that it hurt.

"So that's the ugly story you're running from," she said. "A dead woman, a family history of suicide, and a very elite club." She mimicked his precise pronunciation. "What do you think she's after? Revenge?"

"I did nothing to her," he said, almost savagely. Then the silver behind his eyes slipped away. She touched his cheek, which felt as cool and damp as the window glass. He let her kiss him.

She pauses and asks if you'd like some more wine. Your glass is almost empty. But you shake your head, setting the glass aside, and lift the photograph from the gravel. You see what she means by the mirrors behind his eyes, because they aren't there in the picture. He looks like something made of porcelain and glass.

She found a drawing a few weeks ago, around the side of the trailer, she says. Right after the rain. Doesn't know who could have done it—the nearest house is a mile through the orchard in back, and the highway is twice as far. The picture showed a tree drawn in something brown and gritty, like wet charcoal. Someone was hanging from one of the branches. She thought it might be a woman, hanging by her wrists, wearing a full old-fashioned skirt, but whoever drew it had forgotten to include the head.

But no, she says, there was a head, sticking out under the skirt. The woman was upside down, hanging by her ankles, and her dress had fallen down over her torso, around her grasping arms, her head. It must have been a low branch she was hanging from. Her long hair seemed to coil up on the ground, the ground that the artist hadn't bothered to depict, not even with the straight line of a horizon.

She's not sure what it means, she says. Or maybe she's too sure. Maybe she knows what she wants it to mean, and that's what frightens her: not the knowing or the not knowing, but the wanting.

He stood at the end of the concrete balcony, the very edge of it, the scuffed toes of his oxfords out over the green-blue churning of the Pacific. His arms were folded on the chest-high rail and he was shivering. With cold or excitement, she never knew.

"I wish I knew why she was weeping," he said. He had to shout a little to be heard over the surf, the babble of tourists behind them. "I'd help her if I knew how. Sometimes I think that's why she keeps coming back. She knows I'd help her if I could."

She remembers trying to light a cigarette, but the wind was too sharp and wet. She wrapped her arms around his waist instead, rested her cheek on his shoulder.

"There was a girl back in Massachusetts," he said. "She had dreams, too. Or just one of them. She dreamed she had a miscarriage. Didn't think she was even pregnant, in the dream. Something inside her just died and slipped out."

The next time she delivered the pale orchids to the bookstore, the supervisor at the nonprofit met her in the stairwell. "I used to see you together," he said. "I thought maybe you could see that he gets his things."

He'd been gone for two weeks. Hadn't shown up one morning, didn't return any calls. No one at the address he had on record had ever met an Ethan Phillips. And his desk was exactly as he'd left it, stacked with rejected applications, a photograph of five smiling faces standing between the computer monitor and the jar of neatly marshalled pens. There were three streaks of something gritty and brown on the glass frame.

She never saw him again.

She learned, later, that they had found a girl. Not here—back east, in that weird patch of Cape Ann they called Dogtown, that same summer he'd showed up at the nonprofit in San Francisco. She was hanging upside down from a tree, her hands bound behind her back with duct tape, which was gummed up with dead leaves and pine needles as though it had been dragged some distance over the ground. Twenty-seven stab wounds, at least two of which had hit major arteries.

There were multiple sets of DNA in the short, dark hairs clinging to her sweatshirt, her jeans, in the flakes of skin and dried blood beneath her nails. No matches in any system. But a boy killed himself that autumn, walked into the bay just north of Rockport, and his naked body washed up in a condition that the newspapers declined to describe in further detail. He was, perhaps, the boy on the far left of the photograph, but it's hard to say. They all looked so alike.

The last of the sun slips behind the mountains, and the curve of your wineglass winks in the light of the small, sour-scented candles. Their lanterns and smoke-stained glass jars make a magic circle around her gravel patio, holding back the weight of the dark. This is where it ends, she says, snuffing her cigarette. This is where it ends, this ugly story, at least for her: the white trailer, the bed sheets twisted around her legs some mornings, the taste of metal on the roof of her mouth and in the back of her throat. Longing nested in her abdomen, below her ribs, like an unwanted child she can't carry to term. That's the damned thing about it, this wanting, which has nothing to do, she tells herself, with black eyelashes or candy-colored lips. Nothing to do with what he did or what his eight-times-great-grandfather did or why, or with the bloody-footed thing that follows her in her sleep. Maybe she was always doomed to this toxic kind of restlessness, and the boy with tragic glass eyes was nothing but the occasion.

The Rockport boys, it seems they all disappear eventually. Into the old houses back east that have sat there contemplatively for centuries, brooding over brown rivers with Indian names. Or into the woods, into strange and shadowy Dogtown, or the half-dozen places like it all up and down the coast. Or out to sea.

She tells you the Northern California sun chases away ghosts. The days when she thinks about him, the days like this, are fewer and fewer. Only sometimes in the winter, when the cool rain which comes less and less is sheeting down the windows of the trailer, she feels that longing opening inside her. It's like holding all of space in your stomach, she says. All the stars and planets, all the galaxies. All the emptiness and the cold.

CLEANING UP

TIM WAGGONER

"So that's the grand tour. What do you think?"

The two of us stood in the living room, and I made a show of looking around as if I was considering whether or not to take the job. But of course I would.

The woman was younger than I by about twenty years, in her late twenties or early thirties. She was tall, thin, blond, pale-skinned, and wearing glasses that sat on her face at a funny angle. One slate-gray eye seemed large than the other, and her lips were dry and cracked. She wore a black sweatshirt inside-out and a long hippy skirt that reached to the floor, concealing her legs and feet. She wasn't unattractive, exactly. She was prettier than I was, that's for sure. But an air of unhealthiness clung to her, as if she was one of those people who are always either sick, about to get sick, or recovering from illness.

"Given the size of the house, I'll have to charge ninety dollars a visit. I can come once a week, once every two weeks, once a month – whatever you'd like."

"Once a week would be good. That's how often the last cleaning person came."

The woman's voice was nasally and breathless at the same time, and it sometimes made it difficult to understand what she said. I had no trouble understanding her this time, though, and her words sent up a red flag for me.

"What made you decide to switch cleaning services?" What I was really asking was *What's wrong with the job that made the last person quit?*

She answered a beat too early, as if she'd anticipated the question and had already prepared and rehearsed her answer.

"She retired." The woman added a smile, as if it would make her reply more convincing. Her teeth were yellowed and slightly crooked. They all leaned to the left, both the top and bottom rows.

"Of course," I said, pretending I believed her. Cleaning people—especially those who work for themselves like I do—don't make enough money to retire. They keep working until their bodies can't handle it anymore or until they die, whichever comes first.

The woman—Cheryl Wilson, she'd said when she'd called me—didn't live here. At least, not anymore. This was her parents' house, and she'd called me on their behalf. Her father had a home office in the basement, and he was always super-busy at whatever he did—Cheryl hadn't been clear about what line of work he was in—and her mother was bedridden with some unspecified chronic illness. The "tour" Cheryl had given me had not included the basement or the master bedroom. Those doors had remained closed.

The home was a two-story, three-bedroom, two-bathroom house, with a basement and an attached garage. Family room, living room, kitchen, dining-room, laundry room, attic, deck, and a good-sized yard with several elm trees. In terms of the basics, it was more or less like most of the houses I cleaned. It made me wonder even more why their last cleaning lady had decided to quit. If this size house hadn't been too much for her to handle on her own, maybe she'd quit because of the owners. Some people might've found the situation uncomfortable, working in a house while the residents—whom they'd never met—remained behind closed doors, but I was used to strange jobs.

"When would you like me to start?" I asked.

The woman looked relieved, and more, almost pathetically grateful. She grabbed hold of my hand and gave it a gentle squeeze. Not a handshake, exactly, but something like it.

"Once we've signed the paperwork, you can begin as soon as you like. Right now, if you want."

"That's fine."

We'd left the contract I'd brought on the dining table, so we went into the dining room to sign it. Before we could sit down, though, the quiet was shattered by an ear-splitting shriek that made me jump.

"Don't worry about that," Cheryl said. "Mother does that from time to time. Pay her no attention."

She pulled out a chair and sat, and I did the same.

The next scream that came was louder and longer. Cheryl acted as if she didn't hear it as she perused the contract. This time, I didn't jump. A few screams weren't the worst thing I'd ever experienced. Not by a long shot.

It was the last week of summer break, and I was sitting on the couch, working on the first week of lesson plans on my laptop. This year, I was determined to be ahead of the game when classes started, instead of scrambling like mad to get everything done at the last moment.

I heard the kitchen door open and close, followed by the sound of Ray's bare feet on tile. A second later, I heard water come from the sink faucet, followed by the sound of him washing his hands. He was seventeen, and he'd be a senior this year. I had no idea where he'd been all day. He was too old for me to keep tabs on like I had when he was younger. Plus, he resented my showing any sort of interest in his life. He considered it prying. I figured it was because of what had happened between myself and his father.

So when he finished up washing and walked into the living room, I didn't ask where he'd been or how his day was. I just looked up from my computer, smiled, and simply said, "Hi."

He didn't answer right away. He stood there in an Ohio State basketball jersey and khaki shorts. His skin was deeply tanned from having been outside all summer, and his brown hair stuck up in a spikey cut that all the boys his age seemed to be wearing that year. There was sweat on his forehead and upper lips, there was a look in his eyes that I couldn't read – a mix of fear, confusion, and disbelief. Seeing it sent a chill rippling down my spine.

I closed my computer and said, "What's wrong?"

"I did something bad, Mom. Real bad."

He didn't move, his expression didn't change, but tears started sliding down his face. I hadn't seen him cry since he'd been a child, and it was those tears, more than anything else, that truly scared me.

Once the contract was signed, Cheryl lost no time in getting the hell out of there, claiming she had "errands" to run. "Besides," she added. "this way

I won't be in your hair while you work." She gave me a parting smile and refused to meet my eyes as she left.

I went out to my Prius, folded the contract, put it in the glove box, and then took my cleaning kit from the back seat. I keep my cleaning fluids, sponges, duster, etc. in a plastic carrier, and I held it with one hand while I carried my upright sweeper in the other. I went back inside the house, but I didn't lock the front door behind me. It's reassuring to know I can make a quick exit if I need to.

Since I wasn't supposed to clean the basement or the master bedroom—or go anywhere near them, for that matter—the job would go faster than usual. I started in the kitchen and continued from there. I did my best to make as little noise as possible while I worked. I wanted to be able to hear any noises coming from elsewhere in the house. None did, though – not until I was dusting the family room. It wasn't, as I'd expected, another of the mother's strange cries. She had been quiet since her daughter fled the house. This sound was a soft creaking, as if a door had opened just a crack somewhere. The family room let out onto a foyer which led to the front door, as well as the stairs to the second floor of the house, where the bedrooms and master bath were. But directly opposite the doorway to the family room, just to the right of the stairs, was the basement door. I moved to that end of the family room, even though I'd already dusted there, and pretended to work while I glanced at the door. It was open. Not much, only a couple inches, but it was enough for a strip of darkness to be visible between the jamb and the door's edge. Cool air wafted through the opening, carrying with it a sour smell like an old milk spill on mildewed carpet. I couldn't help making a face at the smell, and I breathed shallowly to keep from inhaling it deeply.

I couldn't see anything through the crack in the door—there were no lights on in the basement where Cheryl's father was supposedly working—but I could feel a gaze settled heavily upon me, and I knew that I was being watched. I heard no breathing, though. Either whoever stood behind the door peeking out breathed so softly I couldn't detect it or he wasn't breathing at all.

I was re-dusting a set of shelves to the right of a flat-screen TV mounted to the wall. Among other knick-knacks on the shelves were several framed pictures of a little girl who was most likely Cheryl. She was alone in the pictures. No Mom, no Dad.

The mother started screaming again, startling me. As if the sound was a cue, the basement door slammed open and a large figure burst forth from the darkness and rushed toward me, the sound of his heavy footfalls covered by his wife's mad shrieking. Hands with discolored sausage-link fingers reached for me, and I thought, *It's about time.*

Ray led me to the garage. The door was closed, and no cars were parked inside. I tended to park my Prius on the street outside the house because I hate backing out of driveways. Ray's car was an old Firebird that perpetually leaked oil, so I insisted he park the damn thing on the street too. The garage wasn't completely empty, though. We kept lawn equipment there, and I had a set of metal shelves where I stored holiday decorations in neatly labeled cardboard boxes. But there was something new in the garage: a body lying face-down on the concrete floor, a halo of blood spreading outward from the head. It was that blood, the sheer amount of it, coupled with the body's utter stillness, that told me I was looking at a corpse. So I didn't rush forward to check for a pulse, and I didn't run back inside to grab my phone and call 911. Instead, I stood next to Ray, who was sobbing openly now, and I struggled to understand exactly what it was I was looking at.

I couldn't see the boy's face, but I could tell that he was around Ray's age and had a similar height and build. He wore a pair of faded jeans with ragged cuffs, but no shirt. He was a bit more muscular than Ray, so I figured he played some kind of sport or maybe was into weightlifting. His hair was short and black, but it might have appeared darker because of the blood soaking it. The back of his head was a concave depression, and I looked at Ray and asked, in a voice far calmer than I felt inside, "What did you hit him with?"

Despite his tears, a calculated look came into his eyes, and I knew he intended to lie. I slapped him—hard.

"The truth," I said.

"I used an axe handle. It's...It's in the trash."

My slapping him had done more than get the truth out of him. He'd stopped crying as well.

"Don't move," I told him, and then—making sure to give the body a wide berth—I walked over to the corner by the garage door where we kept the garbage container. There, lying atop several full white plastic trash bags, was the axe handle, one end covered with thick dark blood and bits of hair. The head had broken off the axe that winter, when Ray had been chopping wood for the fireplace. I'd been after him to fix it, but he'd never gotten around to it. I closed the lid and looked back at the body. A trail of blood spatter led from the body to the receptacle. I looked back at Ray. His hands were clean, and I remembered hearing him wash them in the kitchen before stepping into the living room. Now I knew why.

I walked back to Ray. He was staring at the body, his expression unreadable.

"Who is it?" I asked. I suppose I should've said was.

"Paul Gilman."

I didn't recognize the name. I knew all of Ray's friends, and since I was a teacher in town, I knew many of the other kids that lived in the area, but not all of them.

"He's new," Ray said. "He moved to town at the end of the school year."

"What happened?"

Ray didn't answer right away, and I thought I might have to slap him again to get him talking. But just as I was about to raise my hand, he said, "He sold drugs. Nothing major. Marijuana, mostly. Some pills. Xanax, Vicodin, Percocet, stuff like that. I wanted to buy some off him a couple weeks ago, but he said he was out of supplies. He told me to give him my money, though, and he'd get the stuff for me as soon as he could. I kept checking with him, but he kept telling me to be patient."

"And today you lost your patience."

I'd had no idea that my son was into drugs, but right then it didn't seem important, not with the dead body of his would-be supplier lying on the floor of our garage.

"I called him and told him I wanted my stuff or I wanted my money back. And if he didn't deliver, I was going to spread the word that he couldn't be trusted. He came over to talk, but he didn't bring the drugs *or* my money. We were talking in here, and I got so pissed at him. I saw the axe handle lying in a corner, and then I...I..." He trailed off, his voice flat, toneless.

He didn't need to complete the story. The ending was obvious. I wondered why I hadn't heard anything. Ray and this dead boy had been talking, maybe even shouting at each other. And surely the boy must've cried out when Ray struck him. Unless my son had attacked too swiftly, too savagely, for the boy to have a chance to make any sound before he died. How could something like this happen when I was close by without my having the slightest indication of it?

"I don't know what to do, Momma."

I was startled. I couldn't remember the last time Ray had called me that. *You knew enough to put the axe handle in the trash,* I thought.

I looked at my son. I'd brought him into the world, fed him, nurtured him, taught him, done my best to be both mother and father to him after his dad was gone. And now that boy, who'd once been a smooth-skinned, sweet-smelling baby suckling at my breast, had taken a life. No, that was too gentle a way of putting it. He was a murderer.

"It'll be okay," I said. "We'll *make* it okay."

The duster I was carrying had a wooden handle, and I'd sharpened the end. Instead of trying to flee my attacker, I spun toward him, raised the duster, and plunged the handle toward his left eye. He was naked and fat, with mottled blue-white flesh that looked as if it belonged to some species of marine mammal instead of a man. His body was completely hairless, his scalp covered with thick, throbbing purple veins. His eyes were bulging and bloodshot, the whites yellow, tear ducts oozing black pus. His nose was almost nonexistent, and his lipless mouth was round like a lamprey's and ringed with small but very sharp teeth. The stink that rolled off him hit me like a solid blow, and my gorge rose as I rammed the duster into his eye. The eye popped like an overfilled zit, spraying black fluid that smelled like hot tar. It stippled my hand, face, and blouse, but I ignored it and put as much muscle as I could into driving the handle deeper into the bloated creature's head. He squealed like a hog in the process of being slaughtered, and an orifice opened somewhere in the wobbling flesh folds of his nether regions, releasing a foul-smelling dark liquid. It splattered onto the family room carpet and filled the air with the stomach-churning stench of rotting meat.

He reached up with his sausage fingers and tried to pull the duster out of his eye, but the handle was too slick with whatever substance clogged his veins in place of blood, and he couldn't get a grip on it. I was having similar difficulties holding onto the handle, so I released it, placed both of my hands on the fuzzy end of the duster and shoved hard. I felt a soundless pop as something inside the creature's head gave way, and the duster handle slid further in until the tip encountered solid resistance that I assumed was the back of his skull.

His squeal became a shriek, and he stumbled backward toward the open basement door, pawing uselessly at the fuzzy end of the duster. I ran forward and pushed. My hands sank into his obscene flesh, and I could feel thick liquid sloshing around in there. I imagined he was nothing but a skin sack filled with black goo, and for a moment I feared that his chest and abdomen might explode just as his eye had done. But he was already stumbling backward, and my momentum added to him tumbling down the basement steps. I stood in the doorway, my heart racing, and peered into the basement. The light from the foyer was enough to show the lamprey-mouthed thing lay at an awkward angle on the concrete floor, the veins on top of his head ruptured, and black fluid spread out in a fan pattern behind him. He wasn't moving.

I reached through the open doorway and felt along the wall until I found a light switch. I flicked it and fluorescent lights buzzed to life. I watched the creature for several more moments, but he remained still. Finally, I went down.

The basement was filled with mounds of junk—old furniture, broken TV's, floor lamps missing shades and bulbs, stacks of ancient moldering newspapers. Most disturbing were the piles of discarded clothing, all in various styles and sizes, none of which were large enough to fit the dead thing lying on the floor. Atop one pile was a dark blue polo shirt, and stitched in white letters above the left breast: *Sparkle-and-Shine Cleaners*. I found shirts from several other cleaning companies, but since many cleaners wear their own clothes when working, there was no way of telling how many of these had belonged to members of my current profession. More than a few, I assumed.

The sweet-sour odor I'd detected in the house when I'd first entered was thick down here, and I walked to a closed door on the other side of the basement. I opened it, making sure to hold my breath, and I gazed upon the room's content for several moments, trying to estimate how many people the bits and pieces inside had once belonged to. Eventually, I gave up, closed the door, walked to the corpse—making sure not to get too close to it and keeping a wary eye on it the whole time—and headed back upstairs.

I closed the basement door behind me and listened. I expected the mother to start screaming again, especially after hearing her husband's death cries, but no noise came from upstairs. I went to the kitchen, pulled a butcher knife out of the block on the counter, and started up the carpeted steps toward the master bedroom. I was halfway done. Time to finish the rest of the job.

"Is this deep enough?"

Ray stood in a two foot by six foot hole. The edges were uneven, and the hole only came up to his waist, but I figured it would do and said so.

Grateful to be done, he put the shovel on the ground, climbed out of the hole, and stepped over to stand beside me. It was nearing dusk, but although the sun was low to the horizon, it was still hotter than hell out, the air wet and heavy with humidity. Ray had removed his shirt before starting to dig and sweat poured of his tanned skin. I'd brought several water bottles, and they lay in the grass at my feet. I bent down to grab one and tossed it to him. He caught it, twisted off the cap, dropped it to the grass, then drank quickly.

I looked at the cap lying on the ground. I'd have to remember to pick it up before I left.

While Ray hydrated, I glanced around to make sure that no one was watching—something I'd done at least once a minute since we'd arrived – but I saw no one. My grandmother, Ray's great-grandmother, had passed away a year earlier. She'd left me her home and property—a small house on six acres in the country. The house was empty, but I paid a property maintenance company to keep the grass cut. Not that I could easily afford it on a teacher's salary. There'd been a For Sale sign in front of the house for months, but no one had made an offer yet. Today, that was working in our favor, though. I'd driven the Prius to the back of the property near the fence line. There were a number of trees back there, making it hard to mow, so the grass and weeds were higher, providing sufficient cover for our work. I'd debated whether we should do this now or wait until dusk, but in the country lights and noise draw attention at night since there's little activity to complete with them. I'd decided we'd be safer getting this over with as quickly as possible.

Cleaning up in the garage had been easier than I'd suspected. Some water, bleach, and a couple rolls of paper towels had taken care of the blood. A plastic garbage bag slipped over the boy's ruin of a head, an old carpet to roll him up in, and duct tape to seal him in had done the rest. I'd backed the Prius into the garage, we'd loaded the body into the trunk, and I tossed in another garbage bag containing the used paper towels along and the axe handle. The entire process hadn't taken more than thirty minutes.

"Let's finish this," I said.

Ray nodded, finished the rest of his water, and let the empty plastic bottle slip from his fingers. One more thing I'd had to remember to pick up.

We walked to the rear of the Prius, I popped open the trunk, and together we hauled the body out, walked it to the hole, and dropped it in. The carpet tube made a muffled *thud* as it hit, and Ray jumped. The poor thing was nervous. I didn't blame him. I was too. I had one more task to attend to, and it wasn't going to be easy.

I returned to the car, got the garbage bag, and carried it to the hole. I didn't toss it in, though. Instead, I rejoined Ray and placed the bag near my feet.

"I just don't understand how it happened," Ray said. His gaze was fixed on the carpet tube in the hole. The carpet hadn't been large enough to completely conceal the dead boy's body, and his sneakers stuck out one end. Despite his bemused tone, Ray's nostrils flared as if he were trying to pick up the body's scent from where he stood.

"You couldn't help it," I said. "There's always been a darkness in you. You've gotten in so many fights since you were a child, and we haven't been able to have any pets, not since what you did to the dog when you were nine. You got it from your dad, of course. Once I found out what he was, I shouldn't have married him, but I did. When people started to go missing in the neighborhood, I told myself it wasn't his doing. But it was. And once I found out..."

"You had to clean up his mess," Ray said.

I nodded. "It was my duty as his wife. And after he was gone, I'd hoped you wouldn't inherit his...*inclinations*. But you did."

"I'm sorry, Mom. I guess you have to clean up my mess now, huh?"

"Yes."

I bent down, opened the garbage bag, and pulled out the axe handle. I managed to get a solid grip on it before Ray turned to me, hands now claws, eyes black and cold, barbed tentacles lashing from his mouth toward me. He looked so much like his father at that moment. It only took me two swings to bring him down, and a couple more to finish him. I don't think he could bring himself to hurt me, else it would've been much harder.

I rolled him into the hole with the other boy, tossed the axe handle on top of them, then picked up the shovel and got to work putting dirt back where it belonged.

I opened the master bedroom door, releasing a smell like dead flowers into the hall. I held the butcher knife before me, in case the mother rushed out to attack, but she didn't. I saw why when I stepped into the room. The thing on the bed, sitting with its back against the wall, wasn't simply reclining on the mattress. It was *part* of it. The "bed" was actually an extension of its body. The mother was naked—rail-thin where her husband had been fat—and her skin was a similar blue-white hue as his, but with a grainy texture that made me think of bleu cheese. The bed was made of the same substance, and while it had a suggestion of mattress, box springs, frame, and legs, it grew from the creature's waist—or maybe she grew from it. Her eyes were milky and clouded, like an animal that's lived its entire life underground. His mouth was more human than her husband's, but not by much, and mottled tufts of gray hair clung to her scalp. Instead of hands and fingers, she possessed two long curving hooks, and although I was certain she couldn't see me, she sliced them back and forth through the air, as if trying to warn me off.

The room was bare of any furnishings or decoration. Bones littered the floor, all of them broken, as if she'd wanted to get at the marrow they contained. My guess was that Dad fed first downstairs, then brought up Mom's share for her. He might've been a monster, but at least he'd been a good provider.

Once it became clear the creature presented no threat to me as long as I didn't go near it, I retreated into the hall and closed the door. She started to scream then, but I didn't care. She could make as much noise as she wanted. She'd be quiet soon enough.

I returned to the kitchen, put the knife down on the counter, picked up my cleaning supplies, and went outside. I had several cans of gasoline in the trunk, and after I put my supplies on the back seat, I carried all the cans inside. It took me two trips. I left them in the foyer, retrieved the butcher knife, then sat down on the couch in the living room and waited. Cheryl would return before long to make sure her parents had fed and to get rid of my Prius. But when she entered, she'd find me waiting with the knife. When I finished with her, I'd empty the gas containers throughout the house, taking care to thoroughly soak the basement and master bedroom. I'd light a few matches, toss them, and leave.

I'm so glad I retired from teaching and started my own business. I like being my own boss and setting my own hours, and I get a lot of satisfaction from my work. There's a lot of darkness in the world. I should know: I married a piece of it and gave birth to more of it. But I cleaned up my messes, and now I do what I can to clean up others'. And when I clean a place, I make damn sure it stays that way.

The front door opened tentatively, and I heard Cheryl call out in a hesitant voice.

"Dad? Mom?"

The mother screamed louder than ever, as if trying to warn her daughter.

I rose from the couch, gripped the knife handle tight, and headed for the foyer.

If you're not happy with your present book publisher, try Kraken Press! You'll get the happy blend of perfect horror fiction and rich crime novels that Kraken Press—and only Kraken Press—can give you. Remember, Kraken Press means quality dark fiction. So get complete reading enjoyment.

KRAKEN PRESS
PURVEYORS OF DARKNESS

Deformed Son

JEFF STRAND

"Just so you know, we keep our deformed son chained in the basement," the farmer said. "So when you hear rattling and wailing in the middle of the night, that'll be him."

"Ah," said the traveling salesman. "That's interesting, I guess."

"Now, you may get it into your head that you want to go down the stairs and investigate, but I assure you, when you gaze upon his horrific visage you'll wish you'd done nothing of the sort. He is absolutely disgusting. I mean, simply vile. My stomach hurts a little just thinking about him."

"Not to be rude," said the traveling salesman, "but that's an unusual attitude for a parent to take."

The farmer nodded. "I get what you're saying. And if he were maybe twenty percent less deformed, I'd agree with you. But this kid...let me tell you, when he popped out of his momma, I said 'Shove him back in, he's not done yet.' Normally that would be the kind of thing I'd say out loud and immediately wish I'd kept in my head, but everybody in the delivery room, my beloved wife included, agreed with me."

"Wow."

"We didn't shove it back in, though. That would've been impractical."

The traveling salesman had already wished he hadn't run out of gas on the desolate road in the middle of the night, but this conversation made him wish even more than he hadn't ignored the sign that said "Last Chance Gas Station." He'd figured it was a deceptive marketing campaign.

"Here's your room," said the farmer, opening the door to a small but tidy guest room. "If you value retaining whatever food you've eaten today,

I'd advise you not to leave it. Do not enter any other room under any circumstances."

"What's in the other rooms?"

"Nothing."

"Do you have a daughter?"

"Don't make me regret my hospitality."

"All right. I promise I won't leave the room."

"The obvious exception is the bathroom. You're welcome to leave your room and go into that room if the need arises. I wouldn't deny you that. But otherwise, stay in your room."

The traveling salesman thanked the farmer and went to bed, where he dreamt of a nubile young woman eating a hoagie. Around two in the morning he awoke with the need to empty his bladder. He crossed the hallway and quickly used the toilet for its intended purpose.

After he flushed, he heard rattling and wailing from below.

Did the farmer *really* keep his deformed son locked in the basement, or was this something even more curious?

What kind of traveling salesman would he be if he didn't investigate? He was supposed to be a man of the world, and here was a part of the world he'd never experienced. If he didn't go down into the basement, he'd forever wonder if the farmer had been telling the truth.

As he stepped out of the bathroom, he stood in the hallway for a few minutes, listening for any sign that the farmer might be awake, such as footsteps or muttering. Aside from the wailing and chains rattling, the house was silent.

The traveling salesman decided that he needed to go down there. What was the farmer going to do, stab him through the face with a pitchfork?

He very slowly walked down the stairs to the first floor. Then he crossed through the living room and through the kitchen, until he reached the basement door.

He took a deep breath. Maybe this wasn't a great idea. What if the deformed son was so hideous that the image was permanently burned onto his eyeballs? What if the traveling salesman were, say, about to enjoy a perfectly good hamburger, but instead of the top of the sesame seed bun, he saw only the face of the deformed boy? That would ruin his hamburger.

He should turn back.

He turned around. The farmer stood just outside of the kitchen, looking most unhappy with him.

"I told you to stay in your room," said the farmer.

"Ah, yes," said the traveling salesman. "I do specifically remember us having that particular conversation. What happened is that I woke up, as I often do, confused about my surroundings. I suffer from insomnia and often take a sleeping pill to aid with my unconsciousness, particularly when I'm on the road. So I wandered around the house, trying to remember where I was, until the sight of you just now brought everything back. I suppose I'll head back upstairs now and return to the bed that you so generously provided."

"I don't have a daughter," the farmer said.

"I never suggested that you did."

"That's what you're looking for, right? A sixteen-year-old daughter to ravish?"

"What? Goodness, no."

"You traveling salesmen are all alike. Always looking to score with a farmer's underage daughter."

"No, no, no, sir. Nothing could be further from the truth. Even if she were of the legal age of consent, I would not be creeping around your home in hopes of spending time in her company. That would be disrespectful. It was the sleeping pill. Entirely the sleeping pill."

"Would you be willing to show me the bottle from which the sleeping pill came?"

"That would not be my preference."

"If you're not trying to find my beautiful willing daughter, then the only other explanation is that you wish to gape at my deformed son, which is the behavior of a mentally unstable person. I've said quite clearly how unpleasant he is to the eye. He will turn your dreams into a maelstrom of nightmare images that will forever haunt you. Is that what you want?"

"No, sir."

"Then return to bed, and forget that you ever came down here."

"Yes, sir."

The next morning, the traveling salesman awoke, packed his suitcase, and walked downstairs. "Thank you for your hospitality," he said. "If I might ask one last favor, now that it's daylight, would you drive me to the nearest gas station?"

The farmer took a sip of his cup of coffee and shook his head. "I don't own a car."

"But there's a car in your driveway."

"That hasn't worked in twenty years."

"What about a tractor?"

"Tractor doesn't work, either."

"How do you sustain a farm without a car or tractor?"

"Government subsidies."

"So you have no way of giving me a ride?"

"Nope."

"Is there anything from which I could syphon some gas?"

"Nope."

"How far away is the nearest gas station?"

"About thirty miles."

"That's problematic. I guess I'll have to call a tow truck or something."

The traveling salesman called every auto-related business in the area, and none of them could send a tow truck until the next morning. He was extremely disappointed by this, because every day he wasn't on the road was a day he wasn't selling blenders. The farmer offered to let him stay in his home for another night, and the traveling salesman had no choice but to accept.

"Let me repeat what I said before: do not leave your room. I cannot emphasize strongly enough just now much you would not enjoy the sight of my deformed son. He's got a decent enough personality, but personality can only take you so far, and even the least superficial human being in the country would gag. They might do it discretely, but they'd still gag. Stay in your damn room."

But when the traveling salesman woke up at two in the morning again, he needed to see what was down there, wailing and rattling the chains. What if it was something really cool? He had to know. And though the farmer had been upset with him when he caught him in the kitchen, there was still no reason to believe that it would lead in a pitchfork-through-the-face direction.

What was the worst that could happen?

He very carefully snuck down the stairs, through the living room, and through the kitchen. He placed his hand upon the knob to the door to the basement and ever so slowly, he turned it.

The door was locked.

But it was locked from this side, so he unlocked it.

Ever so slowly, he turned the knob.

He pushed open the door.

The wailing and rattling of chains grew louder, although it wasn't because the actual noise had increased in volume, but rather that the door was no longer muffling the sound.

The traveling salesman suddenly broke into a cold sweat. He'd always prided himself on being a courteous guest, but going into the forbidden basement was more than discourteous, it was flat out rude. If he had a deformed child locked in his basement, he certainly wouldn't want gawkers going down there. He should go back to bed before he saw something he regretted.

No. Not knowing would drive him mad. He'd just take a quick peek.

He flipped the light switch. The wailing abruptly stopped.

Slowly, one step at a time, the traveling salesman walked down the stairs.

A large cobweb-covered curtain hung from the ceiling. The wailing and the rattling of chains was coming from behind it.

The traveling salesman's heart raced. What monstrosity was behind that curtain? How many heads did it have?

Slowly, one step at a time, the traveling salesman walked forward.

He reached for the curtain.

And pulled it aside.

And there, chained to the wall, was a deformed little boy.

He was gross, no doubt, but somehow the traveling salesman had expected him to be even grosser. The boy's eyes, though odd in both color and size, could have been quite a bit odder. It was a nose unlike that which he'd ever seen, yet he'd anticipated a nose that was larger, droopier, and greener. His head wasn't all *that* malformed; you could still get a hat on it if you tried.

There was nothing attractive whatsoever about that little boy. The farmer was right to keep him chained down there. But still, the traveling salesman couldn't help feeling unsatisfied. He'd expected to be forever haunted but instead he'd just be queasy for a few weeks.

Somebody came down the stairs.

The traveling salesman spun around, wondering who the intruder could possibly be.

It was the farmer.

"You fool!" the farmer shouted. "I warned you! I warned you and you didn't listen! You just *had* to look, didn't you? Your sanity isn't doing so well anymore, is it? Is it?"

The traveling salesman shrugged. "He's not as off-putting as I thought."

"Oh. Well...good, I guess. I mean, he's the product of my loins, so if you don't think he looks that bad I suppose it's a compliment."

"He's wretched, don't get me wrong. It's just that with all of the buildup, my imagination created an image that reality couldn't surpass. He couldn't live up to the hype."

"I'm strangely disappointed by your reaction," the farmer admitted.

"It's okay. If you hadn't said anything, and I'd snuck down here to investigate, I'm sure I would have shrieked and crapped my pants."

"Thank you."

"Can we go back upstairs?" asked the traveling salesman. "The way he keeps wailing and rattling those chains is kind of irritating."

"Oh, sure. We should both go back to sleep, anyway."

The next morning, a tow truck arrived and took the traveling salesman to the nearest gas station, where he fueled his vehicle and then went on his way, hoping to have a couple of really strong days' worth of blender sales to make up for the time he'd lost.

He would often look back on his experience in the farmer's home, and each time he did, he'd remember the valuable lesson he'd learned about managing his expectations.

RUST AND FLAME

BRENNEN REECE

Rust & Flame is a storytelling mini-game about a small-time newspaper reporter who travels to the rural South to expose the horrible truth about a vicious unsolved crime. One player plays the role of The Reporter, whose ruthless ambition to get her story may very well be her ruin. The other players play the roles of the townspeople—enigmatic, broken, and dangerous characters with their own secrets and ambitions.

WHAT THIS IS

Over the course of two or three hours, you and your friends collaboratively invent (and act out) a story about an ambitious reporter who goes a little too deep and gets in over her head. You'll probably be more comfortable doing this if at least one person at the table has experience with roleplaying games, improv, or creative writing, but none of this is necessary. I've designed these rules to teach basic storytelling and roleplaying skills.

This is a horror game. That means that it will have horrific elements, not just creepy or atmospheric flavor, and horrible things will happen. The kind of things that make a lot of people dislike the genre. If you might have a problem with the types of situations that can come up, discuss them at the table before playing. You might not want to play this game, and that's okay. It just means that you and the game aren't a good fit for each other.

WHAT YOU'LL NEED

This game requires at least three players. Four is best, and more than five isn't recommended. You'll also need some index cards, pencils, copy paper (US letter or A4), and some regular six-sided dice, which you can steal from almost any board game.

The most important component of this game are the players. Here are some rules to follow to make sure the game goes smoothly. If any of these rules are broken, the players are responsible for the suboptimal experience.

· Turn off your cell phone.
· Don't try to be funny.
· Don't become attached to your character. They're just words on index cards, and are just as disposable.

· Embrace the dark and weird.
· Don't worry about where the story is going, only that it follows logically from what has already happened.

THE BACKSTORY

About year ago, a group of hunters the discovered the smoldering husk of a car on the shoulder of a dirt logging road five miles from Mim's Creek, Alabama. An expensive high-heeled shoe, splattered with wet blood, lay a few feet away from the car.

The hunters sped to the nearest pay phone and notified the police. The police thoroughly searched the woods, but nothing else was found.

Several weeks later, the investigation revealed that the car belonged to Samuel Dunstan, a young preacher from Atlanta who never showed up for his first service at a new church in Mobile. He and his wife Amy have been missing ever since.

After a few months without any leads, the investigation was abandoned.

THE SETTING

Rust & Flame can take place any time from the 1920s to the 1970s. It's important that things like telephones and computers aren't accessible.

The village of Mim's Creek is on the decline regardless of the time period. There's a heavily worn paved road through the cluster of buildings that make up a small business district. Most of the buildings date from before the Civil War, and haven't been properly maintained since.

For the most part, the townspeople are insular, and many of them show signs of inbreeding. Few of them have any education to speak of outside of Sunday school.

You'll find the following buildings and areas in and around Mim's Creek:
· Tavern
· Motel
· Feed & Seed

- Grocery
- Diner
- Pawnshop
- Church
- Cemetery
- Service Station
- Hair Salon
- Town Hall
- Library
- Cotton Mill
- Junkyard
- Swamp
- Woods
- Various farm houses, trailers, etc.
- Anything else you can think of

HOW TO PLAY THE REPORTER

Your goal is to find out what happened to the preacher and his wife, and who was responsible. In play, you'll explore the town and interview the townspeople.

All you have to do is tell the other players what the Reporter does and says. You can be dramatic and use accents if you want, but you can also just describe the Reporter's actions like you're telling a friend about a movie you saw. The other players will describe what things look like, speak for the townspeople, and tell you the consequences of your actions.

ROLLING THE DICE

When you describe the Reporter doing something that might have an unpleasant outcome, one of the other players will tell you to roll the dice. When this happens, roll two six-sided dice and add the results. You'll sometimes add or subtract from this number if the Reporter is particularly good or bad at something, or if one of the other players tells you to do so.

- A result of 10 or higher is a success. This means that you have accomplished what you set out to do. You get the answers you were looking for. You successfully pick the lock of the basement you were imprisoned in, et cetera.

- A result of 7, 8, or 9 is a partial success. This means that you've done what you wanted to do, but it didn't exactly work out the way you wanted. Maybe you got some answers, but the librarian makes a phone call to the sheriff the moment you leave. Perhaps you escape the basement, but on the way out, you knock over some utility shelving and make a lot of noise.

- A result of 6 or less is a failure. This means something bad will happen.

Whatever the result of your roll, one of the other players will tell you what happens next.

Sometimes one of the other players will ask you what you hope to accomplish by taking an action, or they might tell you the consequences if you roll poorly.

If you roll doubles, tell the player playing the townsperson, who will consult "The Hole" and tell you what happens.

MOVES

When the Reporter does something that requires rolling dice, she is making a move.

- Choose one of the following moves that the Reporter excels at. Any time you make that move, add 2 to the result of the roll.

- Choose one of the moves that the reporter is experienced in. Any time you make that move add 1 to the result of the roll.

- Choose one of the moves that the reporter is absolute shit at. Any time you make that move, subtract 1 from the result of the roll.

SNOOP

Sneaking around, hiding, looking for clues, breaking into buildings.
On a 6 or less, you are found out.

ASK QUESTIONS

Interviewing the townspeople about the Crime.
On a 6 or less, your questions are met with somewhat less enthusiasm than you'd have liked. Bad things happen as a result.

RESEARCH

Looking at old newspaper clips at a library.
On a 6 or less, your digging around creates suspicion.

GET OUT OF TROUBLE

Running away from things, escaping from locked closets, untying bound hands.
On a 6 or less, you only make it worse for yourself.

DO SOMETHING STUPID

Climbing walls when the fall could kill you, jumping out of a moving car.
On a 6 or less, you mark 2 Xs.

EARN SOMEONE'S TRUST

Flirting, bribing, buying drinks.
If you earn someone's trust, take +1 to all interactions with them.
On a 6 or less, they, or someone who cares for them, are horribly offended, and you suffer the consequences.

HURT SOMEONE

Shooting, hitting, stabbing.
On a 6 or less, mark an X (see "When you get hurt"). If a gun or knife is involved, mark 2 Xs.

PROPS

The reporter gets 5 undefined props to use at any point in the story. A prop can be anything: a flashlight, camera, Swiss Army knife, lighter, pistol. The only condition is that it has to realistically fit in a purse or messenger bag.

WHEN YOU GET HURT

If, as the result of a move, the Reporter gets hurt, mark an X on an index card. If the injury was the result of a 6-, mark 2 Xs.
For each X, take -1 to any move that requires physical activity.
On the fourth X, the Reporter dies.

HOW TO PLAY THE TOWNSPEOPLE

Take turns playing townspeople. Feel free to play the same townsperson every time they are in a scene, or switch them up.

When you aren't playing a townsperson, it's okay to jump in with details.

DESCRIBE THE SCENE

On your turn describe the scene. Think like a filmmaker. Start with an establishing shot and gradually move to a close-up. Whatever you do, be sure to convey the atmosphere of decay. Target all the senses. Talk about the flickering florescent lights and the flypaper strip and the torn linoleum flooring. The sizzle when the bacon hits the grill and the grease-covered walls. The hand-written advertisements for babysitting or used cars. The roadside bloated carcass of a small dog wearing a pink bejeweled collar.

CREATE THE TOWNSPERSON

Who is the scene's main townsperson? Have we met them before? If not, pull an index card and write down a name and a profession. The profession can be related to the location, but it doesn't have to be.

Describe the townsperson. What's the first thing you notice? The second? The third? Use contrast; if someone is terribly ugly, be sure to provide some beautiful quality as well, and vice versa. The "and" between the second and third qualities should be an implied "but":

The shopkeeper is a morbidly obese middle-aged man with thinning hair and shining blue eyes.

Or:

A barefoot teenaged girl passes you on the street. She has long straight brown hair and her mangled left arm ends just a few inches above where her wrist would have been.

In other words, the people you portray should be just as scarred and decaying as the landscape.

NAMES

Abraham, Byron, Curtis, Damon, Eustace, Franklin, Gordon, Hyram, Ishmael, Lamar, Montgomery, Odell, Quincey, Solon, Waylon, Zachariah

Annabell, Bernice, Clara, Doris, Eudora, Fannie, Gertrude, Helen, Ida, Lemora, Mildred, Oralee, Rebecca, Tori Beth, Willa

INVOLVEMENT WITH THE CRIME

Decide how much the Townsperson knows about the crime, and the degree to which he was involved. Feel free to choose from this list, or roll dice. Either way, mark off your choice and don't choose it again.

· You mind your own business and keep to yourself
· You heard some people talking about it.
· You have been warned not to talk about it.
· You don't know anything about it, and you don't want to know anything about it.
· Your grandmother told stories of similar things happening years ago.
· You remember when this happened before.
· Strangers need to keep their noses out of things they don't understand.
· It happened on your family land.
· You know where the victims are.
· You are close to someone who is involved.
· You were present at the crime.
· You are the high priest.

INTERACTING WITH THE REPORTER

The citizens of Mim's Creek are naturally distrustful of outsiders. When the reporter talks to a Townsperson for the first time, they take a -1 pcnalty.

It's entirely up to you how the Townsperson reacts to the Reporter, but here are some options:
· Ignore them
· Avoid them
· Try to intimidate them
· Act a little too friendly with them
· React violently to them

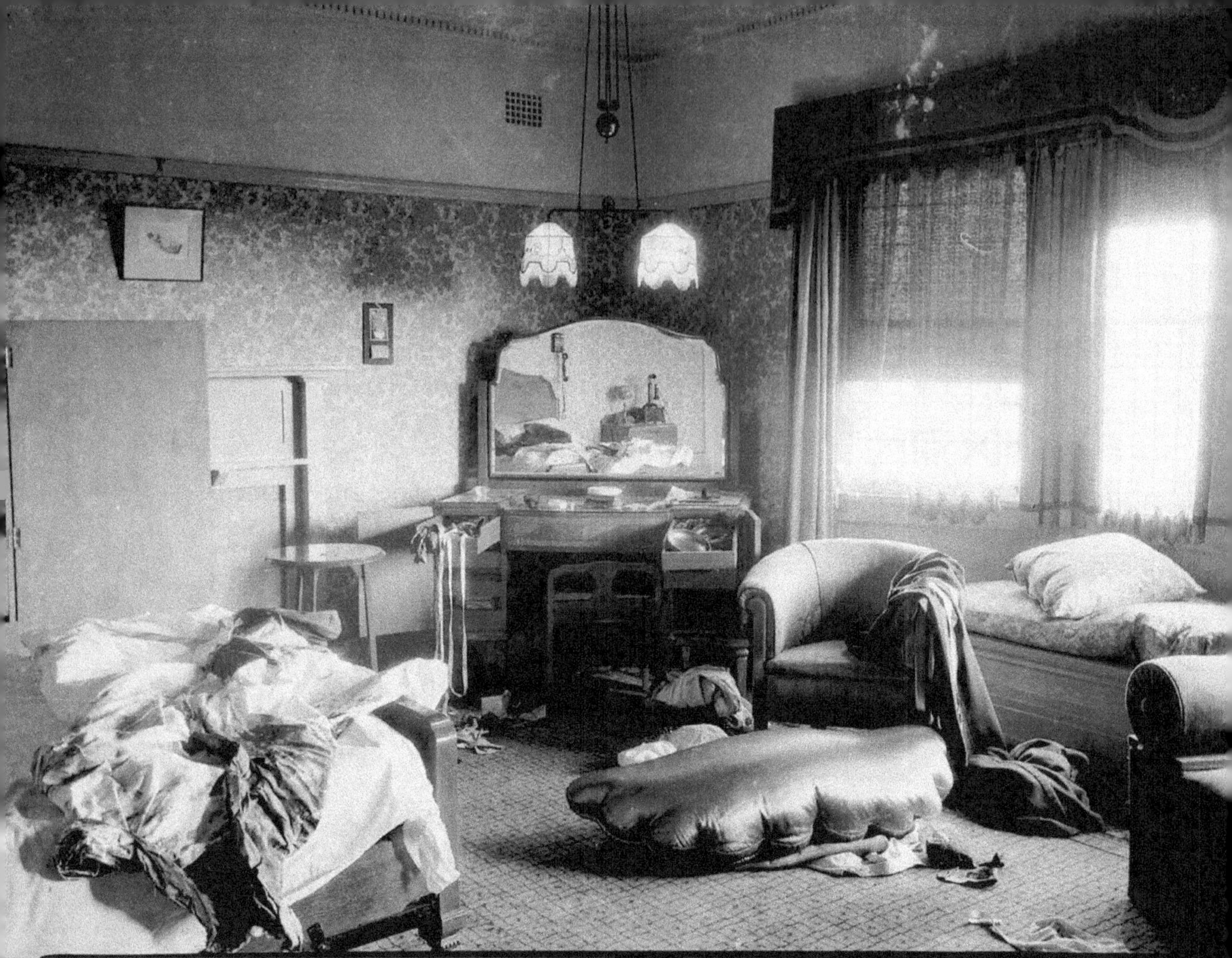

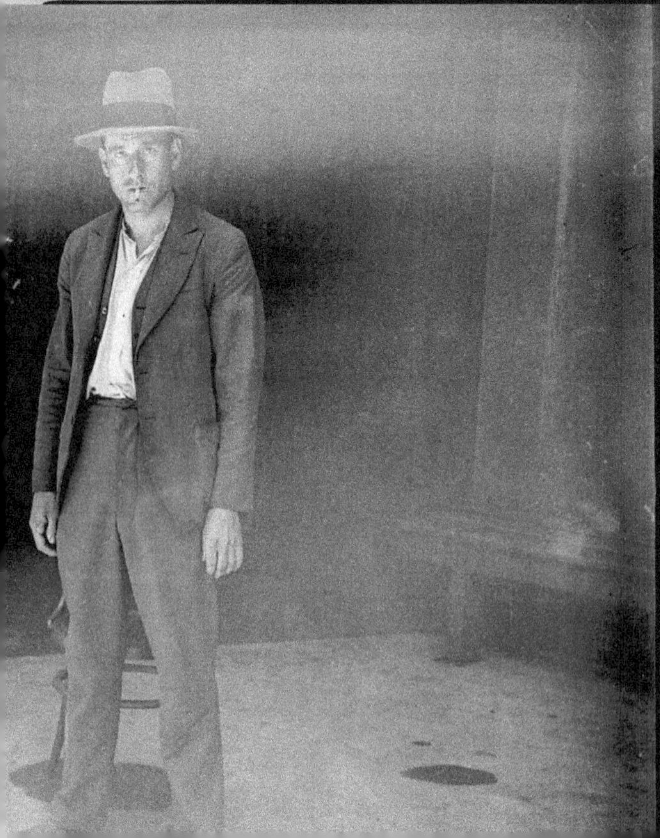

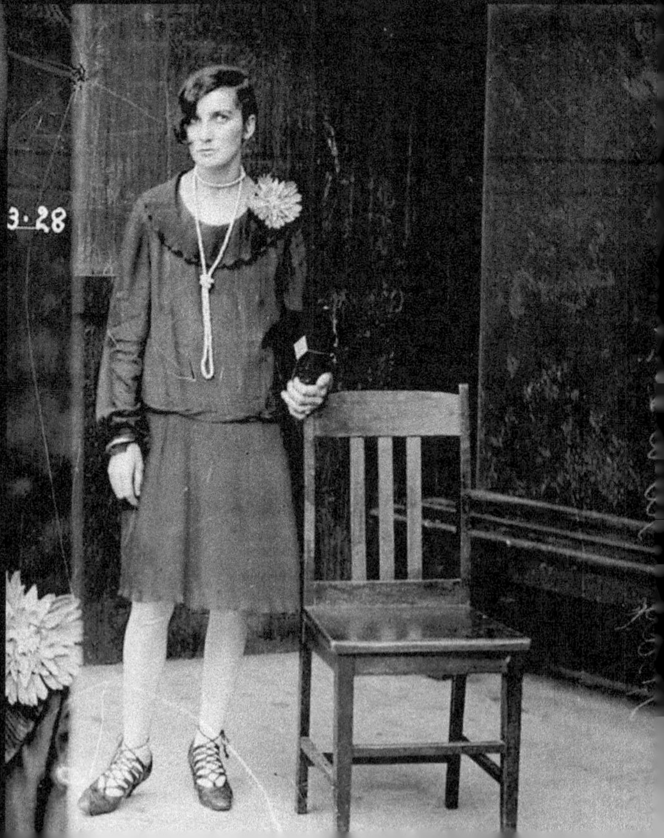
3·28

ENDING THE SCENE

Any player can call for a scene to end. There's no reason to draw it out any longer than necessary. Usually, it's better to call it sooner than later.

THE HOLE

Whenever the Reporter rolls doubles, that is, when the same number comes up on both dice, roll one die and count up to that item on the list. That thing happens, and is marked off.

· A small child stares at the Reporter.
· An old lady crosses the road rather than pass by the Reporter.
· The Reporter is refused service.
· The Reporter's tires are slashed.
· The Reporter finds a dead bird in her bed.
· The Reporter's hotel room has been ransacked.
· The Reporter finds a peephole in her hotel room.
· One of the townspeople you've met has been murdered. It's up to the Town to decide which one.
· A strange man stands on the street, watching the Reporter's hotel room all night.
· The Reporter gets a letter or telegram from her obviously distressed editor telling her to forget about the story and come home.
· The Reporter witnesses something related to the crime.
· The Reporter finds evidence of a similar crime.
· The Reporter witnesses a ritual.
· The Reporter has vivid and disturbing dreams about the crime.
· The Reporter finds shallow graves in the woods.
· The Reporter is taken from her hotel room in the middle of the night.
· The Reporter awakens in a dark room, tied up, and with a nasty headache.
· The Reporter awakens in a deep hole, paralyzed, someone is shoveling dirt into the grave.
· The Reporter finds herself tied to a tree, alone in the forest. Then she notices the approaching shadows…

SOME TIPS FOR PLAYING TOWNSPEOPLE

Don't worry about where the story is going. Just build on what has already happened.

You know something. You're part of this. Either you're trying to get rid of the Reporter, or you are trying to draw her into a trap.

If possible, get into character. Stand up. Look into the eyes of the player who is playing the Reporter and speak directly to them.

WHAT'S REALLY GOING ON HERE

That's for you to discover during play.

There could be some sort of cover-up. Maybe the preacher and his wife were killed during a hunting accident while they were having a picnic in the woods. Maybe there's a cult, and the preacher and his wife were a suitable sacrifice to the old gods. It could be a small group, or the whole town.

Perhaps the preacher and his wife are still alive, being held prisoner. Maybe they're in some farmer's storm cellar; maybe they're in the basement of city hall.

ENDING THE GAME

The game ends when the Reporter is killed or it seems like a good time to end the game.

ARE YOU
THIS KIND OF A MAN ?

We're talking to you regular men, whether you're chained to a desk or work outdoors. You'd rather read some dark fiction than the next airport thriller. Your beard is tough and you find it hard to shave. Kraken Press books are designed for men like you. You can feel it just by looking at the covers. Join the army of "regular guys" who get real dark fiction with Kraken Press. Buy a paperback on our guarantee and read a few pages before bed.

Let our books spark your imagination and captivate your spirit. Make the test tomorrow night. If Kraken Press doesn't measure up to your expectations—return the unread, uncracked paperback to your dealer and he'll refund you nothing.

KRAKEN PRESS
PURVEYORS OF DARKNESS